CREEPY-CRAWLY KILLER

A chilling crime thriller with a stunning final twist

EMMY ELLIS

DI Bethany Smith Book 2

Originally published as *Down in the Garden*

JOFFE BOOKS

Revised edition 2023
Joffe Books, London
www.joffebooks.com

First published in Great Britain in 2019
as *Down in the Garden*

This paperback edition was first published
in Great Britain in 2023

Cover art by Dee Dee Book Covers

ISBN: 978-1-83526-109-5

PROLOGUE

Grief. It lived with you.
Always there. Lurking.

She was dry, so dry. Makeup done, a clown. Hair brushed. Kitted out in the dress James wanted her to wear. He'd bought it from a charity shop, taking ages to find just the right thing. And there it had been, on day four of searching, in all its silky, blood-red glory. A dress fit for a princess.

Except she never was a princess, the dirty slapper.

He stared at her on the floor in his double garage. He'd pick her up in a minute, pop her in the Transit, and take her down in the garden.

That was where all the things had happened to him. The bad things.

Anger should boil inside him, but truth be told, he was fucking knackered, having used that anger already to do what had to be done. It took a lot out of you, didn't it, spending so much energy like he had. Still, there was no going back now. He'd set the ball rolling, and everything had to play out.

Opening the rear door of the van, he tilted his head at what was inside — a single mattress with a cover on it, the ones used for incontinent old people and kids who pissed the bed. He'd attached straps to the sides, two on each. That'd save her sliding off if he took a corner too sharply.

He scooped her up. Soon, she'd be stiff as a damn board, so he'd need to get a move on. With her placed on the mattress and the straps secure, he walked over to the shelving unit where five pairs of shoes sat in boxes. Hers were red, size five. High heels with a glitter effect. Dorothy in the Emerald City.

On another shelf was a bunch of fake gerberas, found in Wilko. He plucked hers out and willed himself not to shudder. He hated these particular flowers — their scent made memories invade, but at least these ones had no smell.

Shoe box and flower beside her, he closed the van doors, blowing out a calming breath.

This was the final part. The drop-off.

He got in the driver's seat and pressed his key fob for the garage door to move upwards, then drove out and clicked again to shut it. A right turn out of his driveway took him towards his destination, and he thought about what he'd done.

* * *

"Say sorry, you bitch."

She hadn't been able to, what with having her face submerged in water.

"Say it like you mean it."

And he'd laughed so hard at that. How could *she say it?*

He wrenched her head up, water dripping off her face, her hair plastered to her cheeks. "Say you're sorry, go on."

She opened her mouth to speak, her eyes wide with pure fear, then he plunged her into the water again, roaring, his fury too much to bear.

Torture. It was what she deserved.

* * *

He reversed onto her drive, not bothered about being seen. Three in the morning was a great time to do your business.

He opened her side gate and took the shoes and the flower into her back garden. Glanced at the houses in the row to check for lights or people awake, nosing out.

Nothing.

Good.

Back at the van, he pulled her out and carried her to where he'd placed the shoes and positioned her beside the fountain. The water tinkled, and he shivered, the sound bringing images he'd rather not see and feelings he'd rather not feel. The air was balmy — this summer had been a bitch so far — and he wiped his forehead with the heel of his hand.

He had to wedge her feet into the shoes, annoyed they hadn't just slipped on like he'd envisaged. He arranged the dress so it fanned out either side of her, then folded her hands over her chest like they did to people in coffins, getting her to hold the flower. He chanced his arm and switched on his phone torch to have a good look at her. She appeared so pale beneath the light. So doll-like.

After snapping a couple of pictures of her, he left, driving away, going home, where he'd get some sleep then begin all over again when he woke up. He had Simon's shirt to iron tomorrow, ready for putting it on him once he was dead.

Killing. Such hard work.

CHAPTER ONE

Under glorious sunshine, Bethany and Mike, her work partner, entered the back garden via a side gate. The property had once belonged to a woman named Ellie White. Thoughts of Vinny, Bethany's recently deceased husband, finally fled her mind. Maybe only for now, but she'd take it. She could focus on this case to get her through the grief. She'd heal with work — that was what he'd want her to do. He'd hate her moping about, pining for him.

Mike stared at the body, his eyes half closed. He cocked his head, seeming deep in thought. "It's obvious to me she's been posed."

"Hmm." Bethany studied the woman, avoiding her face, as that was just too creepy to handle at the minute.

Red dress — the sort worn as a bridesmaid, silky and flowing, the skirt full. Red high-heeled shoes with some sort of glitter all over them. Ellie's arms were crossed, a flower clasped in one hand. It looked like a giant daisy, except the petals were red — to match the dress and shoes? A ladybird crawled on Ellie's bare arm, moving towards her hand, flicking its spotted wings to the sides as though ready to take flight, then changed its mind, drawing them in again to continue its ambling journey.

"Her hair's been styled," Bethany mused.

And it had. Either Ellie had done it like this before death or someone had curled it nicely, the long, dark waves resting on her collarbones. And now for the face. Bethany couldn't put it off any longer. White makeup had been applied, the kind clowns used, giving her a freakish appearance. Thick blue eyeshadow reached right up to the base of her eyebrows, pearlescent and glinting a little from the harsh sunlight. Too much mascara gave the lashes a thick, clumpy effect. Scarlet lips stretched over one of those mouthpieces used in that game where you had to try to say something that made sense. Speak Out, that was it. Her teeth and gums made an unsettling display.

"What the hell does that mean?" she asked, pointing to the mouthpiece.

Mike frowned. "No idea, but that blusher on her cheeks is giving me the willies."

Bethany had to agree. Two perfect pink circles, perhaps made with lipstick. "How old would you say she is?"

"Thirty-odd?"

"That's what I thought."

She glanced around the garden. The body had been placed beside a stone fountain, which sprouted water from the mouth of a naked, female angel with shockingly large chest attributes. It splashed down into a mouldy green pool, creating spreading circles, raindrops in puddles. The area was mainly grass apart from a small patio directly outside the house. A white plastic table and chair set perched on top of it next to a homemade brick barbecue.

Vinny's voice barged into her head: *Stupid to have a barbecue built against a house.*

Bethany's eyes stung. Vinny had been a firefighter and had always reeled off safety advice to anyone who'd listen, eager to save lives even before they were in any danger. She cleared her throat, blinked, and forced her attention elsewhere.

Rose bushes had been trained to climb the trellis nailed onto the blue-painted fences either side, and at the bottom, a row of trimmed conifers provided privacy from the houses beyond. All in all, a neat and tidy oasis, somewhere lovely and calming to sit on a summer day like this one.

Isabelle, the lead SOCO, chatted to a couple of her team members over by the open back door, all of them in protective gear, mouth masks in place, hoods up. Presley, the ME, hadn't arrived yet, and Bethany was eager to know his initial thoughts on the cause of death, because from what she could see, Ellie White didn't have a mark on her.

Unless something sinister lurked beneath that red dress.

Don't let that be the truth.

She shuddered at the memory of her last case, her first serial killer, where a man had gone round carving circles into stomachs, removing the innards, and on two occasions, he'd used a vacuum cleaner to suck out any stray bits. Ellie's dress didn't have bloodstains on it, though, so that was promising.

A photographer snapped pictures of the garden, presumably having already done the body before Bethany and Mike had turned up. She glanced at herself, then Mike, still in black funeral garb from when she'd laid Vinny to rest earlier, although they had booties and gloves on. She was meant to be at his wake in the community hall on her estate, but, unable to face it, and with a call coming in to Mike that Ellie White's body had been found, Bethany had chosen to go to work rather than sit with a load of people offering condolences. If she heard one more 'I'm sorry' today, she'd scream.

Isabelle came over, drawing her face mask down so it rested beneath her chin. She frowned at Bethany. "What are you doing here?"

"Don't say a word," Mike said, holding a hand up. "Beth *needs* to be here."

Isabelle opened her mouth as if to refute that, then snapped it shut again. "Okay . . ."

"Let's just pretend things never happened the way they did. Let's make out I'm absolutely fine," Bethany said, so thankful to Mike for stepping in like that.

He was her rock in the working world, and despite his own sorrow at losing Vinny, his close friend, he still had it in him to look out for her.

"At the moment, I can't stand thinking or talking about it anymore," Bethany said.

"I understand." Isabelle undoubtedly did. Her boyfriend had been killed in the line of duty in Somerset where she used to live, hence the move to Shadwell, to leave all the old ghosts behind. "I have keys to this poor cow's house from a neighbour. Want to come with me to do a walk-through?"

Bethany turned to Mike. "By rights, you're heading the team while I'm on leave . . ."

"But you're no longer on leave," he said and smiled. "You came back to work today as far as I'm concerned."

She'd need to let Chief Kribbs in on that at some point.

"Okay, business as usual then." She sighed out her relief at being able to slip into her usual role. "I need to contact Fran and Leona first to get them going on the victim's searches. Give me two minutes." She walked away, towards the barbecue, and rang the incident room. "Hi, Fran, it's me. Before you say anything, I'm back at work today and don't want to talk about . . . about Vinny."

"Okay, whatever you want."

"Just act normal. I can't stomach any more pity. Okay, we have a body. An Ellie White, eighty-four Bawden Avenue. Can you and Leona do your usual, please?"

"Will do."

"Thanks. I'll message you if we have more before we return to the station, and you do the same if you find out anything I need to know. There's a neighbour we need to speak to, so we might be a while." She ended the call and waved at Isabelle and Mike.

They joined her, then Isabelle led the way inside through the back door into a kitchen. Minimal. Clean. White, like the deceased's surname.

"Did you get much info out of the neighbour?" Bethany asked Isabelle, glancing around to check for any signs of a struggle, any blood on the walls or floor.

Nothing.

"Only that they're good friends. She said Ellie had a date last night, although Ellie didn't open up as to who it was with." Isabelle shrugged. "The neighbour's called Sunbeam Drayton, can you believe."

"Oh . . ." Bethany smiled. "Is she all airy-fairy?"

"I'll let you see for yourself." Isabelle grinned. "She lives two doors down at eighty-two. Right, I've been through the house already, and a few of my team are still working in here, but early indications show this isn't a crime scene, just the garden."

They checked all the rooms, and Isabelle was right. It was obsessively tidy, although that could be a red flag. Maybe the killer had cleaned it thoroughly.

Back in the garden, Bethany approached the newly arrived Presley, who stood filling out his usual scene form where he'd no doubt sketch the position of the body on it.

He jolted upon seeing her beside him. "Work's the best medicine for you then." He smiled. "I can't see anything obvious here, I'm afraid, so you're going to have to wait until I get her on my table." He nodded at Ellie. "Her makeup's a bit over the top, isn't it? Or is that how people go about these days?"

Mike joined them. "Probably significant, although at the moment, I have no clue as to what it means."

"Me neither," Bethany said.

Presley knelt beside Ellie. "Thickest sodding lashes I ever saw, even for fake ones."

Bethany frowned. "I just thought she loved overdoing mascara. Maybe she has two sets of falsies on." She peered closer.

Presley ferreted in his bag and took out an eyeglass. He leaned over Ellie and looked through it. "Oh, someone's either got too much time on their hands or is leaving you a little clue. They're not lashes. More like spiders' legs or something like that."

Bethany jumped back in recoil. "What?"

"Come and see." Presley gestured for her to get down there with him.

Did she really need to do that? "Um, no. I'm not a spider fan. Here's my phone. Take a picture, will you?" She popped in the passcode.

He took it, accessed her camera, and moved close to capture an image. Shielding the phone with one hand — that damn sunlight — he said, "Yep, that'll do." He passed the mobile back.

Bethany steeled herself to look at the screen. Mike positioned himself to block out the sun, bless him, and she stared down. A blue eye filled the frame, and yes, they were definitely legs of some kind, all black and furry, jagged strips instead of the usual lash arcs. "Looks like they were glued on." She shuddered. "So we have someone who doesn't mind plucking legs off spiders or whatever and spending quite a while attaching them to the victim. For them to have done this, it has to mean something, surely. Otherwise, what's the bloody point?"

"Unless they did it for kicks," Mike said.

"Some people are sodding weird," she muttered.

"Um . . ." Presley cleared his throat. "She has an earplug in her right ear. The sort you use on planes to stop take-off pain."

Bethany bent over and, sure enough, the yellow circular end of a plug greeted her. "What the hell? Is there one in the left?"

"No." Presley took a small plastic tub out of his bag, the kind he put small pieces of evidence in that came off bodies. He placed it beneath her ear and, using tweezers, pulled out the plug.

A flurry of dead ants spewed out, some landing in the tub, others on her neck.

"Fuck me." Bethany stood upright and moved back a step. "What the chuff are they doing in there?"

Mike shook his head. "This is one sick bugger."

"I'll just check the other side." Presley dropped the plug into an evidence bag, then picked up his slim torch. He shone it in the left ear. "Ah, looks like a dried-out slug, albeit a small one."

Bethany blinked at the news, then held back a squeal as a worm slithered out of Ellie's nostril. "Dear God, how long has *that* been in there?" She covered her mouth and shivered.

Presley bagged the slug and worm separately. "May as well check at the back of the mouth . . ."

"Do I even want to know?" Bethany asked no one. She swallowed, her skin prickling at the sight of all the creepy crawlies.

"She has no tongue, but something else has been left there." Presley used longer tweezers and plucked out a blue plastic butterfly, the sort that might have once been on the end of a stick for people to poke into their flowerpots.

"Oh . . ." Bethany scratched her head — it felt like nits scurried over her scalp. "Well, this is more than I expected."

She drew her phone out and sent a message to Fran:

> CHECK FOR ANY COMMONALITIES WITH THE FOLLOWING, APART FROM THE OBVIOUS: ANTS, SPIDERS, SLUGS, WORMS, BLUE BUTTERFLIES. I'LL SEND YOU A PICTURE OF A FLOWER IN A SEC AS WELL. WE NEED TO KNOW WHAT IT'S CALLED.

Isabelle strolled over. "What's going on here then?"

Bethany told her about the bugs.

"Are they in those bags?" Isabelle asked.

Presley nodded and handed them over. "I haven't written the info on them yet."

"No worries." Isabelle smiled. "Just quickly sign your siggy in the appropriate boxes, and I'll sort the rest. These can be taken down to the lab then. The quicker we do that, the better."

Presley did as she'd asked, and Isabelle walked off with the evidence. Bethany snapped an image of the flower and sent it to Fran. Hopefully, something would come of it, though Bethany wasn't holding her breath.

Fran's message came back:

> Fran: ELLIE WHITE'S PARENTS LIVE IN CYPRUS. I'VE CONTACTED THE AUTHORITIES THERE TO INFORM THEM OF HER DEATH. SHE HAS NO SIBLINGS. WE'RE STILL LOOKING INTO AUNTS ETC. HER FACEBOOK IS BUSTLING, SO IT'LL TAKE US A WHILE TO SIFT THROUGH IT.
>
> Bethany: OKAY, THANKS.

She sighed and looked at Mike. "With all the bugs and the flower, and what with her being placed here," — she pointed at the grass — "I'd say we have a garden theme going on. It's not rocket science, is it."

"What's with the dress, the sparkly shoes, the makeup, no tongue, and that mouthpiece, though?" He rubbed his temples.

"Something we need to find out," she said.

Presley held up a hand. "Time of death, rough estimate, sometime last night. Her temp indicates about eleven p.m., but with this humidity . . ."

"Okay, cheers." She turned back to Mike. "Come on. Let's go and speak to this Sunshine woman. Maybe she'll have some information we can actually use."

"Sunbeam," Mike said.

"Same thing, isn't it?" Her stomach growled, something that hadn't happened much since Vinny's death. "Then we'll go and get some lunch afterwards." She frowned. "D'you know, no one has texted me asking why I'm not at the wake. While I'd be pissed off if they did, it's annoyed me that no one seems to give a toss. I know, I'm contrary, but still . . ."

Mike smiled gently. "That's because I messaged Vin's brother and told him you couldn't face it and to spread the word not to contact you for a few days."

Her eyes misted up, and a familiar lump took up residence in her throat. "You're so good to me."

"Yeah, well, it goes both ways."

They stared at each other for a while, unspoken words floating between them, and she wanted to hug him, fighting off the urge to break down.

No. Chin up. Keep yourself on an even keel.

She nodded briskly then led the way down the side of the house, disposed of the gloves and booties, then went out to the street, discreetly wiping away the tears that insisted on coursing over her cheeks.

Damn them.

CHAPTER TWO

Sunbeam Drayton was as far from a hippy as she could be. Her name didn't match her appearance, and Bethany chastised herself for even presuming the woman would be floating around in a flower-print, wavering skirt, a tie-dye vest top, and toking on a reefer, telling them to chill and be at one with nature, man. She resembled a gym bunny in her black Lycra leggings and cerise top, a pair of light-pink Nikes on her dainty little feet. Her blonde hair, scraped up in the tightest ponytail Bethany had ever seen, swung from side to side as she walked down the hallway after letting them in.

In a kitchen at the end, she grabbed three cups, put coffee and sugar in them, then used an instant hot water machine to make the drinks. "Have a seat," she said, gesturing to the breakfast bar.

Sitting there would mean they'd be in a row, and Bethany wanted to study Sunbeam's face while she questioned her, so she indicated for Mike to take a pew while she stood opposite. Sunbeam added milk then handed the drinks out.

"Not resting your legs?" Sunbeam asked Bethany, as chirpy as you like.

Doesn't she care that her friend is dead?

"No, thank you. I prefer to stand, but you feel free to join Mike there." Bethany smiled and picked up her cup. The coffee tasted wonderful.

Sunbeam sat on a stool and drank some of hers, too. "Ah, this is heaven. How do people live without this stuff, eh?" With no reply from either of them, she said, "What do you need to know about Ellie?" She didn't appear to have been crying, so either it hadn't hit her yet or she wasn't the sobbing type.

Or perhaps she's a sociopath.

Mike took his notebook out.

Bethany jumped right in. "Where were you last night?"

Sunbeam chuckled. "Ooh, this is just like on the telly."

Bethany frowned. Was this woman all there? "Can you answer the question, please?"

"I was out getting drunk," Sunbeam said, "with a friend called Cathy Grant. I can give you her number and address if you need to check? She only lives down the road a bit."

Bethany nodded, and Sunbeam rattled it off, Mike writing it all down.

"What time did you leave your house?" Bethany asked.

"About six thirty. I went along to Cathy's, and we had a bottle of wine between us, you know, to save the pennies while we were out. It was her birthday, so we'd both booked today off. Hangovers and all that."

"What time did you arrive home?"

"About midnight. We started off at the local — The Gift Horse's Mouth, d'you know it? Anyway, we ended up getting a taxi into the city and spending the rest of the night at Shard's, the new nightclub, and oh my God, that place is banging." She presented the back of her hand. "I've still got the entry ink stamp on me. It takes ages to get them off, doesn't it."

No idea, love . . .

"Okay. Did you notice anything irregular when you got back? And how did you get home?"

"Taxi again, straight from Shard's — didn't fancy a kebab or whatever; I think I'd have thrown up — and no, I was too pissed to see anything except my front door, and even then, I had double vision. You know how it is."

Bethany didn't, but there you go. "When did you call the police?"

"Well, I overslept this morning, didn't I. Woke up at about eleven, maybe five past, then I had a shower and got dressed. I'd planned to go to the gym, but that police lady in the white outfit told me to stay at home." She peered at the ceiling, thinking, then looked at Bethany. "Hmm, so it must have been about quarter to twelve? I opened my curtains in the bedroom — mine's at the back — and saw Ellie on the grass, the daft mare. I went down to go and see her, see why she was even there — she had a red dress on as far as I made out — but another neighbour, old Polly at number eighty-seven, stopped me out the front for a natter and said she'd been annoyed last night by some bloke driving up in a Transit van."

Bethany's heart lurched in alarm. "Did you tell the other officer, Isabelle Abbott, about that?"

"No. Should I have?" Sunbeam blinked. "Anyway, Polly asked me what I was doing, and I said: Going round Ellie's. She's on the grass in the garden. So Polly said: What do you mean? And I said: Well, looks like she's out for the count, sunbathing in a bloody ballgown of all things!" She paused for breath. "And, you know, what with this sun and how hot it's been, I didn't want her getting burnt. Polly said, because the van had been at Ellie's, and Polly had also seen her lying in the garden, that we'd better ring the police. So I did, although why you need to be here for someone who's sunbathing is beyond me. Is she all right?"

What? "Ellie?"

"Who else?" Her plucked-within-an-inch-of-their-life eyebrows shot up.

"So Isabelle didn't pass on any information to you then?" *Call me stunned.*

"No . . ."

That explained why this woman was bubbly and unaffected by her friend's death — she didn't even sodding know about it.

"Okay. Um, Isabelle said you mentioned Ellie was going out on a date last night but that she didn't say his name. Did you see anyone come to collect her?"

"No, afraid not. I was long gone by the time she was due to leave. She said she'd be going to Mezzo's for about eight, meeting him there. The Italian restaurant that costs about a tenner just to eat an olive."

Not a place where a red bridesmaid type outfit would be needed.

"The dress Ellie had on. Have you seen it before?" Bethany sipped her drink.

Sunbeam shook her head. "That's the thing, you see. Ellie wouldn't be seen dead in something like that."

The silence following Sunbeam's titter hung heavy.

"I mean, it's a scream!" Sunbeam laughed again, clearly not catching the uneasiness in the air. "Just you wait until I see her. I'm going to rip the piss out of her."

"Did Ellie mention anything *at all* about her date apart from what you've told us?" Bethany pressed.

"No. Oh, hang on. It's someone I know, that was all she'd give me. A bit mysterious, but that's Ellie all over. She likes intrigue."

"Do you have someone who can come and sit with you at all?" Bethany may as well get this on the way to being wrapped up.

"What for?" Sunbeam cocked her head, frowning.

"Do you know of anyone who would want to harm Ellie?"

"Ha! Not likely. She's a doll."

Mike glanced at Bethany, and she caught on to what he'd picked up. Ellie's makeup, how she looked doll-like. She gave him an imperceptible nod. Was he thinking Sunbeam was dropping subtle hints, thinking she was clever and they wouldn't realise she was the killer? Bethany didn't think this woman had anything to do with Ellie's death, though, but you just never knew.

"Right, back to you having someone to sit with," Bethany went on. "Do you?"

"I can always get Cathy round here, I suppose, but why you want me to sit with someone is beyond me." Sunbeam lifted her phone. "Shall I message her? She can be here inside two minutes."

"Yes, please." While the text was being sent, Bethany enquired, "How long have you known Ellie?"

"Since we were kids. We met in year five when she moved to Shadwell."

This was going to hit Sunbeam hard then.

"What sort of person was Ellie?" Bethany waited for Sunbeam to clock the past tense.

"She's great. Funny, caring, do anything for you. An example of that is my car broke down, so she paid for it to be fixed until I got my wages." Sunbeam paused. "Come to think of it, I still owe her twenty quid. I must give that to her."

The sound of a key sliding into the lock had Bethany peering out into the hallway. A slender woman, short brunette hair, with shadows under her eyes entered the house and jumped upon spotting her.

"That'll be Cathy," Sunbeam said. "We have keys for each other's places." Then she called out, "In here, woman!"

Cathy came into the room and jolted again at seeing Mike. The keys in her hand jingled. "What's going on?"

"I didn't tell you in the message — too much typing," Sunbeam said. "You know it hurts my thumbs. This is the police. Ellie's in her bloody garden wearing some well nasty dress, and for some reason . . ." Her face fell, and she gazed over at Bethany. "Why *are* you here?"

Mike got up so Cathy could sit. He came to join Bethany opposite the two women.

"Cathy, can you confirm where Sunbeam was last night?" Bethany asked.

Cathy recited a similar story, although she couldn't remember what time they'd got into the taxi outside Shard's — 'too off my face'. It didn't matter. CCTV would sort that.

"Do you know Ellie well?"

Cathy shook her head. "Not really. She's Sun's friend more than mine, although we have gone out a couple of times as a trio. Ellie isn't my cup of tea. Too quiet. She doesn't go out to get rat-arsed like we do, does she, Sun?"

"No, she's more of a single cocktail girl, making it last all night," Sunbeam said. "Remember when she had a Mai Tai and we reckoned it must have been warm by the time she finished?"

Cathy laughed. "Gross."

Bethany took a deep breath. She needed to close this down so she could go and see this Polly woman at number eighty-seven. "I'm so sorry to have to tell you, but Ellie was murdered last night."

Cathy whacked a hand over her mouth to stifle a squeal.

Sunbeam blinked, clearly in shock. "No, that can't be right. She's sunbathing in the garden."

Bethany glanced at Mike and gave him a pleading look: *Please deal with these two* . . . He gave them minimal information, and once the women had taken it all in amid tears and hiccups, Bethany and Mike left the house. She led the way to eighty-seven, and an elderly woman with a snowy perm stood out in her garden, staring along the street at Ellie's house, squinting to see through her gold, thin-framed glasses.

"Polly, is it?" Bethany asked, holding up her ID.

"Yes, Polly Dilway . . ." She wrung her gnarled hands, the skin rasping.

"I'm DI Bethany Smith, and this is DS Mike Wilkins. Do you have a moment?"

"Of course. Come in. It must be about Ellie . . . Yes, that's it."

She ushered them up her path with a waft of her hand, then into the house, the musty smell cloying. In a living room that was wall-to-wall clutter — shelves full of dusty ornaments, books, magazines, candles, and dried flower arrangements that had seen better days — they sat, Polly on a lilac velour wingback chair, Mike and Bethany on a floral sofa with sagging cushions, complete with circle divots where various bums had perched there over the years.

Bethany smiled. "Mrs Dilway—"

"Miss." The old girl frowned, her white eyebrows drawing low.

"Begging your pardon. Miss Dilway, can you tell us when you first saw Ellie in the garden?"

"First thing. I'm up with the lark — it's the angina." She rubbed her chest for emphasis.

When the hell is the lark awake? "What time was that, exactly?"

"Six."

"Did you not think it strange that a young woman was out there at that hour?"

"Not really. People do weird things these days, don't they. You've only got to turn on the telly to know that." She shrugged and sucked on her lower lip, then let it flop back out. "She could have been doing that meditation business, bonding her soul with the elements and all that. Did you see *Nature's Call* the other night? Well, some people, they have sex with the *earth*." She shook her head. "Have you ever heard of the like? They think they'll be saving the planet by doing it." She nodded. "So, yes, I thought she might be up to something like that."

Okay . . . "What about the Transit? Tell me about that."

"My chest was playing me up about quarter to three — would you like a drink?"

"No, thank you, we've just had one." Bethany smiled. "Carry on."

"As I said, my chest . . . I got up, made a cuppa, and took it back to bed with me. I heard a right old rumble, like an engine was on its last legs, you know, and went into the front bedroom to have a look out. It was a white van, and they'd parked it up outside Ellie's, on the drive. Well, they'd reversed, I should say," Dilway said. "Took a box from the back and went round the side of her house, so I just thought it was one of them late-night delivery drivers."

"What did you do then?"

"I went to bed, drank my tea in the dark, and drifted back off."

"So you got up again at six, yes?"

"Yes, and that's when I saw her after opening my curtains."

"Did you look out at her again after that?"

"No, I thought if she was doing the rudie thing she'd appreciate some privacy. Besides, I had breakfast to make, then I managed a shower — I have one of them chairs in the bath so I don't slip; they're a godsend. By the time that was done, I got the bus into town and was there a good couple of hours — there was a market on, and I needed me veg. I met my friend for a cuppa and a slice of cake, then, as I was walking down the street to come home, I saw Sunbeam — and isn't that a silly name? — going round to Ellie's. And it struck me, when Sunbeam said Ellie was *still* in the garden, that she'd been there for far too long, and what with the Transit . . ." She pushed her specs up her nose. "I have to admit I'm not too good in the brain department these days, and it took a while for the old noggin to catch on to the fact that something wasn't right. I should have realised that when Ellie was out there first thing this morning."

"Don't worry." *It wouldn't have made a difference if you'd rung us earlier. Ellie would probably still be dead.* "Did you see the driver clearly?"

She leaned forward then shifted about to get comfortable. "They were a silhouette. Their head almost reached the top of the Transit roof, if that helps. A tall bugger."

"Yes, that helps a lot, thank you. Have you ever seen the van down here before?"

"I couldn't say if it was that particular one — people drive them all the time, parcel men and whatever — but a white van did park opposite mine for about an hour last week, and no one got out."

Excellent. "Did you see the driver that time?"

"Afraid not. It had one of them sunshade wotsits on the side window, the sort you get for kiddies. Black, it was, although I suppose you can see through them from the inside. They're like mesh, that sort."

"Do you recall what time he arrived?"

"After them *Loose Women* had been on the telly."

"Thank you. Miss Dilway, you've been most helpful. We'll let you get on now."

Bethany and Mike left before Polly could ask any questions about Ellie. Their next stop was buying some lunch, Bethany's treat, but before that, she walked the length of the street from end to end to check for home CCTV. Shit out of luck. Then she had a word with the uniforms doing door-to-door. Satisfied they hadn't found anything useful from the neighbours yet, she got in the car and waited for Mike to join her, then drove off, her stomach complaining that her throat had been cut.

CHAPTER THREE

James hummed to himself along with the tune coming from the wind-up jewellery box. He'd listened to it as a kid when locked in the shed at the bottom of the garden, watching the ballerina turn around and around, one arm curved above her head, her tutu plastic and stiff. *Bring on the Clowns.* Such a haunting melody, one that had kept him sane.

He ironed Simon's shirt, ready for tonight after they'd met up for a bevvy. Simon was a right dickhead, and James had never liked him, although he'd pretended for the sake of the others in their group that he did. Simon was one of those sorts who walked around with a can of lager no matter what time of day it was, a roll-up — be it tobacco or weed — clamped between his thin lips. Some people held fags with their teeth, didn't they, but not this bloke. He only had one left. The rest had gone manky over the years, falling out, either through lack of brushing or going rotten, James wasn't exactly sure. Simon was due to have new ones soon, courtesy of the NHS.

Shame he wouldn't be getting them.

Good. It'll save the taxpayer from footing the bill.

"But it *isn't* a shame, is it, Pretty Princess," James said to the ballerina. He laughed, hysteria creeping up on him.

He pressed the iron to the shirt collar. Steam rose along with the scent of charity shop clothing he hadn't been able to get out no matter how many times he'd washed it at sixty degrees with Ariel and Lenor. "None of them deserve my friendship. They're all a bunch of tossers." Like Ellie, they'd soon realise that by taking the piss out of his secret, they wouldn't be alive to do it to anyone else.

Simon's cheeks grew hot along with his anger. He hung the shirt up on a hanger over the kitchen door, then put the iron and board away. The suit he'd bought for Simon had been dry cleaned, so that was one less thing for James to do. He'd washed the red tie by hand.

He thought about Ellie and how she'd been all coy when they'd met up in the alley beside Mezzo's — he'd checked out the CCTV and couldn't wait for her in the street or he'd have been spotted.

He was glad she was dead.

One down, four more to go.

* * *

"What have you done, James?" She stared down at him, that aunt of his, her fleshy cheeks florid, streaked with tiny red veins from the drink.

He didn't dare break eye contact — that wasn't allowed — but the image of what he'd done was right there in his head, a floating, mocking reminder. "I dropped the flour."

"Yes, you dropped the flour." She bunched her fists and propped them on her hips, her meaty arms bowed at the sides. "But what else have you done?"

He struggled to think. As far as he knew, that was the only bad thing today. "I don't know."

"What you've done," she said, gritting her slim, yellow-orange teeth with gaps in between, "is not clear the fucking mess up."

His heart hammered, and he told himself not to pee. Not here, not when she was in front of him. He'd get a clout for it, and maybe a kick up the backside, too.

"What shall I do with you?" She pressed a finger to her lips and tilted her head. "I know. Come with me, down in the garden."

It was dark out, and winter, and going in the garden now meant he'd get cold. He wondered why she'd want to take him there at six in the evening but didn't ask. Since she'd taken him to live with her after his mother had died — he didn't have a dad — he'd been scared of her.

"I don't bloody want you or like you, just remember that," she'd said on the day he'd moved in holding his scraggly teddy in one hand and a small, battered suitcase with the other.

He remembered thinking: I don't like you either — and I want Mummy back.

She grabbed his wrist, startling him from the past, and yanked him towards the back door, flinging it open and power-walking him to the bottom of the grass where a shed stood surrounded by flowerpots that didn't have anything pretty in them at the moment. The darkness was almost absolute there, too far away from the light spilling from the house, and something snuffled about in the undergrowth, probably one of the hedgehogs she fed cat food to.

The water fountain tinkled.

"Stand there," she said, clamping her heavy hands on his shoulders.

He wished he was sixteen so he could leave, not seven, where he was stuck with her, living a life of fear. Tears stung, and he blinked to send them on their way down his face. They were hot until the snap in the air tried to freeze them.

"Don't move until I say you can."

She left him then, barrelling up the path to the door, then disappeared inside to close the curtains, blocking out the welcoming glow.

He stood there for ages and ages, shivering, afraid, and at one point, a nasty moth batted at his head, the wings getting caught up in his fringe. James shrieked and flapped it away, sobs wrenching out of him. He sniffed and swiped at the tears, and in the end, he couldn't hold his wee any longer. Out it came, seeming to burn his legs, then going super cold as the winter evening wrapped its frozen fingers around his thighs, his shins, his feet.

Eventually, his whole body numbed, the tips of his ears hurting from the low temperature. More snuffles sounded from the area beside the shed, and he promised himself it was the hedgehogs, it really was, not a man who'd been waiting for this moment to snatch him away to an even worse life.

Could there be one? Was there someone out there more hideous than Auntie Angelica, with her overly large nostrils that flared every time she got angry with him, that quivered with each slap she landed on his face, his head, the backs of his legs?

He didn't think so.

This was like that place called Hell that Angelica had told him about, where she was the Devil, and he'd be going there if he kept doing bad things.

The curtain snapped to the right on the back door, then she thundered down to him, grabbing his arm. He barely registered her fingernails digging in, his skin so frigid.

"Inside," she said, dragging him along behind her.

The warmth of the house enveloped him in a hug, and she locked them in.

"Get over to the table and eat your dinner." She pointed to where their plates had been set out.

Hers was full.

His was empty.

"Well, go on!" She shoved him in the back.

He stumbled over there and sat, his legs tingling from the heat coming into them. As was usual when he'd been what she called a 'naughty noodle', he went without his main meal and had to sit there and pretend he was eating it. Enjoying it.

How could you enjoy air?

She crashed down onto her seat and attacked the chicken pie. It had been his job to make the pastry, but with him spilling the flour and then . . . and then going out there . . .

Tears left searing tracks down his thawing cheeks.

One day he'd get out of here.

One day.

CHAPTER FOUR

The hair of the dog Simon had been drinking all day had done nothing to get rid of this morning's hangover. Christ, his tongue seemed to fill his mouth, and if he didn't know better, he'd say it was covered in sand. That was unusual, feeling so shitty, because he drank about twelve cans of Foster's a day, and it hadn't affected him like this for years.

He had to go out later to meet up with James, which was odd, considering the bloke couldn't stand him. Oh, James hid it well, but Simon knew better and had done since they were kids. Still, free booze was free booze, and that was what James had offered, a good old lads' night out in the city centre. What was it in aid of, though? And why hadn't James asked their other mate, Gavin, as well? It would have been a better get-together then.

His phone rang, and his ex's name popped up on the screen. He ignored it — she probably expected him to do something daddish, and he didn't feel like it. She'd basically brought their three young sons up alone, seeing as he liked the drink too much, and while he'd been able to help moneywise for around three years when he'd had that good job at the biscuit factory, he hadn't contributed an awful lot — cash or otherwise. She said he didn't care about any of them, that he was a waste of space, but fucking hell, tell him something he didn't know. His mother said the same thing.

He glanced at his watch. Four o'clock. Yeah, Natasha would be home from school with the kids by now. What could she be after? Maybe she wanted to bend his ear about child support again, but with him being on Job Seekers, he just about had enough cash to keep himself stocked up on what he needed, let alone the kids. And anyway, she was a social worker, and they earnt a shitload, didn't they? She could provide for their boys well enough, even though she said her wages weren't all that. He reckoned she was just pretending on that score.

Rather than ring her back to find out what she wanted, he walked the few streets to her place, preferring to wind her up in person. He waited for a flurry of texts from her — that was what she'd always done in the past — but lately she'd taken to not doing that. It bugged him. He liked watching her anger grow with each text she sent. It gave him a sense of power that he was controlling her, even though they were no longer together. Annoying her was one of his favourite pastimes.

At her door, he knocked and waited. The giggles of his boys filtered out of the open living room window — sounded like they were having a right old time of it, laughing at something on the telly. Probably *Paw Patrol* or *PJ Masks*.

Natasha opened up and stood staring at him through the six-inch-wide gap.

"What did you want me for?" he said, all casual, then glanced down the street to the little shop at the end as though everything was hunky-dory.

Whenever he came here to spy on her down the alley opposite between two houses, she sometimes nipped to Buy on the Go to get the Diet Coke she loved, and he'd swear she was shagging the owner, Bazza. She talked to him at the counter for at least thirty seconds, and that had to mean something, didn't it?

He gave her his attention again, shoving one hand in his pocket and lifting his Foster's to take a long swig. He burped in her face.

She glared at him, opening the door a bit more. "If you'd answered your phone, you'd know what I bloody wanted, wouldn't you?"

He grinned, flashing his gums and his lonely tooth. "Well, I'm asking now, aren't I? My battery's low, that's why I didn't take your call." He was such a good liar.

"I needed you to watch the little ones while I took Archie to the dentist, but it doesn't matter now."

"Why doesn't it matter? Bazza coming to look after them, is he?"

She frowned as though he was mental. "Who the fuck is Bazza?"

Oh, so she was playing that game, was she? Making out she didn't know who ran the shop? Well, he wasn't having any of that. He'd get her to admit it if it was the last thing he did.

"Don't pretend, you slag. He's the geezer you're with now, and don't tell me he isn't, because I know it's true."

"What?"

"Bazza. The bloke in Buy on the Go."

"*Him*?" Her eyebrows rose. "I didn't know that was his name, and I don't even *know* him like that."

"You must do. You talk to him a lot." He weaved his torso from side to side, chuffed to bits with himself. That had shocked her, hadn't it.

"How do you bloody know?" she said. "Have you been watching me?"

Shit. He'd gone and put his foot in it. If she thought he'd been spying on her, she'd keep an eye out for him in future and catch him at it. Best he steer the subject elsewhere. "Do you want me to have the kids or not?"

Natasha shook her head — one of those pity shakes, like he was the lowest of the low. "No. Go away."

She slammed the door in his face. He was used to that now, but it still stunned him every time she did it. Ah well, she'd come around again eventually. In the meantime, he had James to get drunk with, and that beat seeing his kids any day.

Simon trotted down the road, glugging his beer and wondering whether James would spring for a kebab after they'd got pissed up. Wouldn't hurt to suggest it, would it?

With the idea of a doner filling his belly, he whistled and went home, looking forward to getting a few vodkas out of his old mate an' all.

* * *

Everything was prepared for later, so James sat at the kitchen table and ate some homemade chicken pie, the memory of his first time left out in the garden triggering his need for comfort food. He could make out that night hadn't gone badly, that his tiny belly hadn't been empty and hadn't growled all night, reminding him again and again that he hadn't had any dinner. He pretended he was that little boy again and chewed the pie, acting as though he hadn't gone without on that night so long ago.

Just because he could, while he'd made the pastry, he'd spilt the flour again. There was no Aunt Angelica with her massive nostrils to tell him off or send him into the garden. No, she was long gone, and good bloody riddance. The bitch had died of natural causes, more's the pity. Annoying, because he'd planned to make her his first kill but, as usual, she'd had the last laugh, passing from a random heart attack.

Still, she was gone, that was the main thing.

Shame she still lived on in his head.

He finished his meal then went up for a shower, and afterwards, he slung on his dark clothing and popped on a black baseball cap. With his boots the last thing to sort, he was ready. In the garage, he got in the Transit with its purposely mud-splattered number plates and reversed onto the street, closing the garage door with his key blipper.

He drove to the city and parked down a side street that had no CCTV, just a few higgledy-piggledy houses butted up against each other like old mates having a drunken hug. He suspected Simon would be half cut already, seeing as he sank multiple beers throughout the day, but then again, he was probably an alchie by now and the drink had minimal effect.

Head down, James navigated the backstreets surrounding the main hub of the city until he came to the alleyway beside Branner's, the trendy bar that sold cocktails. Ellie used to like going there for a Mai Tai. Maybe he'd have one at some point and toast the bitch in Hell. He'd hoped her death would have been on the news by now, but so far, nothing.

He peered around the wall of the building to take a look at the outdoor drinking area, penned in by a low, decorative trellis fence with fake ivy all over it. Inside the square it created, people sat on rattan furniture with cream cushions, the fancy sort for gardens that cost a bomb. Simon stood in one corner, eyeing up the tables, probably so he could walk past later and swipe a packet of fags, the thieving bastard.

James whistled their group's call from childhood, and Simon glanced over and smiled, showing his usual black cavity with a mouldy tooth that no longer had any buddies. James' stomach rolled.

Revolting twat.

He beckoned Simon over, and together they walked down the alley.

"Where are we going?" Simon asked, his halitosis wafting out.

James stopped breathing for a moment, then, "My house." He dipped his head again and pulled his cap brim lower.

"I thought we were going out on the lash," Simon whined, tugging a can of beer out of his lightweight jacket pocket.

"We were, but I thought it'd be better doing it at home. You can smoke weed then, can't you — but only in the garden." That almost had him laughing, considering what he had planned for later.

"All right, but only if you order a takeaway as well. I'm sodding starving, me."

"Whatever. I've had my dinner, but you can buy whatever you want. It's your money after all."

They weaved through the streets, James waiting for Simon's usual excuse.

"See, that's the thing . . ." Simon opened his can.

"Don't tell me. You don't have any money." James gritted his teeth.

"Hang on, that's a bit fucking rude." Simon chugged down some beer.

"True, though, except you always manage to find it for booze, fags, and dope. It'd be better spent on your lads, don't you think?"

"Natasha's got all that in hand. And anyway, it's none of your business."

Once news had got out regarding Simon's death, James would take some cash round to Natasha. "Come on, get in."

They'd reached the van, and James unlocked it.

"And don't drink that on the way. Coppers could see you. They might not allow passengers to drink alcohol." He got in and started the engine, eager to get on with this now. Simon got on his last nerve at the best of times, but right at this moment, the bloke was skating on seriously thin ice.

At his house, James led the way inside via the internal door in the garage. Simon smelt like a brewery, and James had to breathe through his mouth until they got in the kitchen. He slid a bottle of voddy along the worktop, a glass swiftly following, and watched in disgust as Simon threw half a glass down his throat then poured another.

"You not having one, eh, J?" he asked, taking out his baccy tin and preparing to make a rollie.

"In a bit," he lied. "But go steady, eh? That's Grey Goose you're drinking, not Tesco Value."

Simon shrugged, clearly not giving a monkey's chuff how much the vodka cost. "Tastes the same." He rolled his fag with his tobacco-stained fingers and licked the paper. "Do I still need to go outside if it's just a ciggie?"

James nodded. "Yep."

Simon disappeared through the back doorway, coming to stand on the patio, facing away from the kitchen window.

James studied him and had the violent urge to go out there and grab Simon's hair, drag him to the ground, and slam his head repeatedly on the slabs. Best not to, though, seeing as it was still lightish and people might be having a cold glass of wine in their gardens. They'd hear Simon screaming.

While the drink-addicted wanker smoked, and although James knew damn well everything was in order, he still had to check again. He ran into the garage, pleased Simon hadn't noticed the table with the special thing he'd used with Ellie to drown her slapper self in. Simon would see it soon enough, though, and James had no doubts about his 'friend' getting drunk, which would help the process. Ellie had refused any alcohol, which had made it a tad difficult to get her to tell him what the others had said behind his back about his secret. She'd kept her mouth shut right to the end. Even forcing her face into the water hadn't made a blind bit of difference.

Why hadn't she said sorry? Why was it so hard for her to do that? If he'd been the one coming to the end of his life, he'd sure as shit say it.

But you didn't give her the chance to.

I know. Be quiet, you.

He checked the water level in his piece of kit and, satisfied it was full enough — although he had spare flagons under the table to top it up if need be — he returned to the kitchen. Simon wasn't standing outside the window anymore, and James got annoyed. What was he doing? Snooping round the house to see what he could nick and sell down at Cash Converters? Simon was always mentioning James' wealth and how it wasn't fair that he was rich and Simon wasn't. Like James had said to him once: I work and earn it. You sponge off the social.

"Simon?" he called out in the hallway.

The toilet by the front door flushed, and the pisshead came out.

"Did you wash your hands?" James asked, pointing at them.

Simon tutted and went back in the loo. His voice floated out. "Have you always been so womanish or what? And who has such a posh toilet anyway? Oh, I forgot, I'm in James' house, the man with everything."

I don't have everything, though, do I — no nice childhood after Mum died, no lovely memories once that fucking Angelica got hold of me.

James stifled the need to rush in there and smack Simon's face into the mirror over the sink, the broken shards digging into his creepy little eyes, blinding the bastard. "It's unhygienic," was all he managed to say. If he wasn't careful, he'd blow this. He was getting a bit irate.

Calm down. Get another drink in him, then he'll blab.

He waited for him in the kitchen, and Simon swaggered in, the Grey Goose in his system giving a waver to his steps. Simon was such a grotty sod. It looked like he hadn't had a shower or washed his clothes for ages.

"Here," James said, pouring another vodka, but only halfway up the glass this time.

Simon flung himself onto a stool by the island and sipped, wincing at the burn of alcohol. Funny how it hadn't bothered him before.

"When are you buying me that takeaway then? I'm really hungry now, like, hurting hungry."

"In a minute." James planned to do no such thing. "Can I ask a serious question?" He held his breath and told himself not to react while Simon picked his nose.

Not yet. Save the anger for later.

"What sort of question?" Simon wiped his finger on his jeans.

So help me God . . . James passed him a piece of kitchen roll. "Don't be fucking grim," he snapped, dogged off by being in his presence. He needed to get this done so he had time to fix Simon's face up before he dumped him.

Simon cleaned his jeans and put the tissue in his pocket. "Are you going to answer me or what? I *said*, what sort of question?"

"You know when I told all of you what had happened to me as a kid?"

"Yeah?" Simon sniggered, the twazzock.

Did you expect anything less?

James pressed on. "Did any of you talk about it amongst yourselves afterwards?"

Simon shrugged. "Look, mate, I was well drunk that night, as you know, and by the time you'd stormed off, I'd fallen asleep on the sofa, so if the others discussed it, I didn't hear them." He laughed for a moment too long, his mouth open, his single tooth brown and manky, hanging from his gum like an old stick. "Did you really used to piss yourself?"

James clenched his jaw. This bloke . . . no wonder he'd never liked him.

"You ought to apologise for that," James said. "And for laughing at me on the night I told you all."

Simon sucked down the rest of the vodka in his glass, then slammed it onto the island. "I don't have to apologise for jack shit. It's not my problem you were locked in a fucking shed when you'd been a *naughty noodle*."

James saw red.

CHAPTER FIVE

Simon was on the floor in the garage beside the Transit. James had dragged him in there, out of the blue, punched him in the stomach, and watched as Simon had fallen backwards, cracking his head on an old-fashioned Welsh dresser that had cans of paint and garden tools on the shelves. It had really hurt. There was no call for this sort of crap. James must be off his rocker.

"What the fuck?" Simon shifted onto his knees and rubbed the egg-sized lump on his scalp. "There's no need to get shitty, is there?"

"There's every need." James' face had gone well red. He must be angry. "I told you something horrible, and it took guts to do it, too, and every single one of you found it amusing. How do you think that made me feel?"

The lump on Simon's head throbbed, and he took his hand away from it to check for bleeding, but there was nothing. He had to be careful how he answered. James was in a right old state, and if Simon said the wrong thing, he could find himself on the end of a nasty beating. It wouldn't be the first time. He'd had a fair few scraps with James when they'd been kids, one in their late teens, when James, bigger and stronger, had knocked Simon out. The thing was, that

Goose shit he'd been drinking had muddled his head, and even though this seemed to be turning into a dire situation, he still had the need to laugh. What was that all about?

Nerves, most probably.

"Look, we were all lashed up to the eyeballs that night," he said, hoping that excuse would be enough. "Maybe we thought you'd made it up. Maybe the idea of you wetting yourself, you know, with you being so up your own arse these days, we imagined you doing it as an adult, and it struck a funny bone. Either way, it wasn't our fault you had a fucked-up auntie, was it? I mean, what did you expect us to do about it after you'd told us your turdish little story?"

Well done, Si. That was really being careful with what you said.

"You could have given me some sympathy, at least." James' eyes were so wide they must be straining.

"What? Sympathy? You're a big boy now, J. Shit happens. Deal with it." Seemed like watching what he was saying had gone right out of the window. "Anyway, if she was that bad, why didn't you tell a teacher or ring the police?" He stood, wobbling, his sight going blurry. "If it was so awful, you'd have done anything to get away from her, wouldn't you? I mean, who the hell sticks around when they're being abused?"

"You have no bloody idea, do you?" James closed his eyes for a brief moment, then stared at Simon — too hard and for too long. "You didn't listen to a word I said that night, did you? I *explained* why I couldn't tell anyone at the time. Being in that sort of situation isn't easy. You're too afraid to do or say anything to the person who's dishing it out. They're frightening, yet at the same time they're all you know." James balled his hands into fists, his biceps flexing beneath the tight sleeves of his black T-shirt.

Crap. He's going to get nasty again. "I didn't hear that bit, I swear."

"Say you're sorry."

Despite his need to diffuse the situation, belligerence crept into Simon. He didn't like being forced to do or say stuff, and a small part of him acknowledged that James had

had to do that as a kid. Still, Simon opened his stupid mouth before his brain had fully engaged. "No. I'm not saying sorry for what you went through — that wasn't down to me. I didn't treat you that way."

A muscle in James' jaw ticked. "I don't expect you to say sorry for *that*. It was the laughing. For how you lot left me feeling. It took balls to tell you all and look what you did. You treated it as a fucking joke."

"Oh, come on. It was funny, man. Admit it. If one of us had told you the same thing, you'd have laughed an' all. You had some mental aunt who liked putting spiders and things on you. It's amusing."

James lunged at him, giving him a shove good and proper, and once again, Simon went sprawling into the dresser. Paint cans toppled to the floor, one of the lids flying off, the blue contents splashing. A set of secateurs whacked him on the head, but luckily not the pointed end.

James wrenched the hair at the back of Simon's head and forced him towards an old-fashioned teak table that stood against the right-hand wall.

Is that a foot spa on it?

Opening his mouth to ask that very question, Simon had no chance to speak. James flicked a switch on the side of the spa, and bubbles frothed about inside it, the machine humming. Then his head was shoved down, and he found his face submerged. He foolishly sucked in air, inhaling the water, and choked, heaved, his lungs straining. A buzzing set up home in his ears, reminding him of a million flies and, oddly, he thought of the story James had told them about the bluebottles in the shed.

He swung his arms around in an attempt to push James away, ineffectual in his desperate need to get out of this situation. The bottom of the spa was blue, and it gave him the sense he was drowning in the sea. That brought on terror, and he fought harder.

James tugged his hair, and Simon was free of the water. He gasped, never so grateful to be able to breathe. He gulped in more oxygen, vaguely catching the fact that James was speaking.

"Say you're sorry! Tell me you didn't mean to laugh."

Water fell from Simon's fringe into his eyes, and he shook his head to make the strands move away, but they were plastered to his forehead.

"Is that a no?" James said, close to his ear, his breath hot on Simon's skin.

With no time to explain the miscommunication, Simon watched the spa come up to greet him again. Face plunged inside, he gagged and managed to hold his breath this time, his cheeks heating, the bubbles thrumming a mad, disjointed tattoo on his face, some going up his nose. He managed to get a grip on the table edge and push, but James was too strong and held him in place, so Simon bent his knees, ready to drop to the floor. But blackness crowded his mind, panic setting its feet firmly in his chest when he realised time was running out, and his legs went stiff with fear, the bastards. He strained to rear his head back, desperate to be free of the water, but he was stuck there by James' strong hold.

Darkness overtook him.

* * *

James stared down at Simon. The prat had stopped breathing, but James wasn't finished with him yet. As he'd done with Ellie, he sank to his knees and, despite having to put his mouth on Simon's disgusting lips, he began CPR. He wanted to hear the magic words — *I'm so sorry!* — and that meant bringing Simon back to life.

A rib cracked.

It didn't take many breaths and chest compressions. Simon coughed, just like they did on the telly, just like Ellie, and James hefted him onto his side. Water seeped out of his mouth, the gurgle meshing with the ones the bubbles created in the spa. Simon blinked, and it was so clear he was confused as eff and had no idea why he'd be staring at an old dresser and paint cans on the floor.

James let him fall onto his back and loomed over him. "Awake and alert now, are we?" He pulled away, stood, then leaned down and hefted the manky little shit to his feet. "Say you're sorry."

Simon must have got some fire in his belly. His eyes blazed, and his mouth skewed into a sneer. "Fuck you! You expect me to say sorry when you drowned me?" He raised his fist and threw a punch.

James darted to one side, and Simon, with his dripping hair to match his drippy personality, missed. He went to throw another. James offered a slug of his own, right in Simon's guts, and his 'mate' doubled over, wheezing and grumbling.

"What the fuck is *wrong* with you, J?"

"I just want an apology. Is that really too much to ask?"

It wasn't, was it?

Simon, still bent over, said, "I'll never say sorry to you, so save your breath from asking."

James rushed around Simon to stand behind him, grabbed a fistful of his hair again, and dragged him over to the spa. This fucker was going to *learn* to say sorry. He forced Simon's face into the tumultuous water. The stupid twat's arm swings were useless in getting James to stop. All it did was fuel him, spur him on to get what he wanted. He'd longed to hear those words for years from Auntie Angelica, and she'd always refused to say them, too. What was the *matter* with people? Didn't they see that he just needed some sort of confirmation that what he'd been through was wrong? Why was him being locked up in a shed funny? What sort of friends did he have if they'd laughed about something so hideous?

They're not friends at all. Not true ones.

You've got no one in your corner.

Simon stopped pratting about, giving up on his efforts to break free of James' hold. His body went limp, but James kept him where he was in case he was pretending to be dead, expecting James to let him go. He waited for the count of sixty seconds, then placed him on the floor.

CPR. A slap to his cheek. Simon breathing again. Lifted to his feet by his hair.

"Say. Sorry. To. Me," James said. Begged.

Simon spat in his face.

Back to the spa.

No more CPR.

* * *

Pretty Princess spun on her stage, the melody twinkling out while James worked. Simon was dry now, so dry, his whole body clean from the sponge bath James had given him on a sheet of plastic on the garage floor. He'd styled the wanker's hair so he actually looked decent for a change. For once in his sorry, shitty little existence, Simon appeared nice in that suit, not like some tramp. James had always been embarrassed on Simon's behalf for the way he didn't care about his appearance. All he'd cared about was his mates called Foster's and Smirnoff — if his Jobseekers ran to buying that brand of voddy.

The white makeup had been applied, signifying James' fear in the shed or at the bottom of the garden. He'd always imagined he'd appeared ghostly back then. Why hadn't the neighbours seen him out there, his pale face hovering in the darkness? Why had no one rescued him?

Those thoughts gave him the impetus to continue, so he wedged in the mouthpiece and popped in a plastic butterfly, blue like Ellie's, the same as the one that had batted at his face that time one summer when he'd been forced to stand there under the raging sun from noon until three.

He'd fainted from heatstroke.

The eyelash extensions were ridiculous on Simon, but they had to be there regardless. They reminded James of another time, but he'd prefer to forget about that for the moment. In one of his ears he placed dead woodlice, and in the other . . . he didn't want to think about that either.

Simon was ready.

James got up and stared down at him. Anyone would think the bloke was getting married, what with his fancy clothes. James picked him up, putting all of his effort into it, and dumped him on the mattress in the van, then collected Simon's shoebox and gerbera from the shelving unit. With Simon strapped in place, it was time to leave him in his garden at the crappy one-bed he rented in the shabbier part of Shadwell.

Maybe *this* body would make the news.

* * *

Auntie Angelica's nostrils flared again, which only meant one thing. She was angry. Ready to teach him a lesson and make him understand how much she hated him. He understood all right, she'd made that clear on countless occasions, so why did he need the constant reminders? She only looked after him for the money Mum had left for his care.

"Out you go," she said, pointing to the back door, her cheeks red.

He dutifully went, hoping that if he obeyed, she'd see he was a nice boy really, like Mrs Kavanaugh at school thought he was. She said he was kind for sharing the toys, and that he was gentle with the children who were shy and didn't mix well. In truth, James was shy himself, but at school he pushed it to one side, desperate to be noticed as a good boy, someone who wasn't a 'bastard', 'brat', or that C-word Auntie sometimes used. She said he was a naughty noodle, but wasn't she one for swearing at him?

In the semi-darkness — it was about six o'clock, early autumn — he walked over the grass and waited for her at the shed, just in case she wanted him in there this time. Seemed she did, because she slid the padlock key into place and opened the door. He stared at the interior, which was completely bare of any garden tools or the usual paraphernalia, the window boarded up with a square of plywood. The only thing it contained was a jewellery box on the floor. She'd swept away the bugs from before, although spiders clung ominously from webs in the corners, waiting to dangle down on their silky threads and crawl all over him.

He shivered.

"Get in." She shoved his back.

He stumbled forward, tripping over the lip at the bottom of the doorway, and landed on his knees.

"Move into your corner."

He obeyed, tears gathering, but he wouldn't let them fall. If she saw them, she'd call him a 'snivelling wretch of a twat', and he didn't like hearing those words. He settled in his usual space and waited for her to bring in what she always did. And there she was, in the doorway holding white tubs with thin metal handles. She took a torch out of her pocket and switched it on, placing it in another corner so it illuminated the space. Then she closed the door, not that he would ever try to run out.

He didn't know what he'd done wrong, but he must have done something for her to be doing this again.

"Now, this evening we have new little friends for you. Would you like to see them?"

He nodded, even though he didn't want to, but that was the response she expected. If he didn't give it, in the past she'd pinched the skin on his tummy and twisted it so hard he'd squealed and cried. It had left a terrible bruise which had gone from purple-blue to greeny-yellow over the course of a fortnight. Mrs Kavanaugh hadn't seen it when he'd changed for PE because he'd left his vest on.

Auntie Angelica took the lid off the white tubs, and he didn't dare peer harder to see what was in them. That would become clear soon enough. But at least it wasn't moths or butterflies — they'd have flown out by now and fluttered all around him until he was sick with fear. He hated them so much.

She lifted one tub and walked over to his corner, and he held his breath, knowing what was coming next. She poured the contents into his lap, and he stared down at what must be thousands of beetles, their backs shiny with a green tint, their legs scurrying over his, up his stomach, some heading for his face. He held back tears, whimpers, and anything that would encourage her to be more wicked to him.

"Aren't they pretty?" she asked, cocking her head and staring at him.

He nodded again.

"They'll keep you company, as will these."

She brought the other tub over and emptied it on his head. The smell was revolting, and so many of the nasty creatures wiggled on him, their white bodies plump.

"These are maggots," she said, "and the man at the fishing tackle shop told me they're almost ready to turn into pupa. Do you know what that means?"

He shook his head, keeping his mouth closed so nothing crept in there, breathing through his nose, his nostrils flaring like Angelica's did. And, God, he hated to be anything like her.

"It means they'll stay as a pupa for about three to six days, and then they'll become flies. You'll be happy to know you can come in here and meet them once they've all hatched. You'd like that, wouldn't you?"

He opened his mouth for long enough to say yes, then snapped it shut again.

"Enjoy your time in here. And remember, if you move, I'll know. I always know."

He had a feeling she had a camera in here somewhere. She must do, otherwise, how could she see him?

She picked up the torch and switched it off, then exited the shed. The sound of her locking him in brought on stomach spasms, and once he'd left enough time for her to have walked up the garden and into the house, he puffed out a sigh of relief.

He reached for the jewellery box and wound it up, opened the lid and imagined Pretty Princess doing her beautiful ballet dancing. The tune soothed him for all of thirty seconds, then his mind switched to what was going on with the bugs.

More beetles made their way from his lap to his face, his hair, and they shuffled around on him, their tiny feet scuttling over his skin, whisper-light but at the same time heavy.

One climbed into his ear and burrowed.

And he let the tears fall but didn't scream.

No, he wasn't allowed to do that.

Pretty Princess danced on.

CHAPTER SIX

A new day, one that would see Bethany and Mike interviewing a few of Ellie's friends. They'd already spoken to Sunbeam Drayton, of course, but yesterday, Facebook had provided the information that Ellie had belonged to a gang, although not the sinister kind. This one was just a group of kids growing up together from year five right through to now. The others on the list were Gavin Yates, Simon Knight, James Obbington, and a Yazeem Thomas. They had their addresses and places of work, thanks to Leona doing her usual digging, and it was just a case of turning up and hoping they could speak to them.

Bethany hadn't slept too well the night before. The bed seemed so bloody empty without Vinny in it, more so than the times he'd been on the night shift. But that had been different. She'd known he was coming home at some point and would get in beside her, hoping she didn't wake, but she always did. He usually smelt of sandalwood from his quick stint in the shower to wash off the scent of smoke or just him freshening up from sitting around if they hadn't had a call-out that night. She'd got up bleary eyed and hollow-chested again and supposed that was her new normal.

And it fucking hurt.

Time to get on with it, though.

"Which way round do you want to do these?" she asked Mike, sitting beside him at his desk.

He'd been working out a route to save them scratching their heads about where to go while they were out in the city. "Yazeem Thomas works closest, so we'll go there, shall we?"

"Okay. She's in that office block along the way a bit. What does she do again?"

"Estate agent, so we might miss her if she's out at a house." Mike picked up his notebook where he'd drawn a crude map and written the locations. "Are you okay?" he asked quietly. "What did Kribbs have to say when you went in to see him earlier?"

"I'm fine; he was fine. Surprised I'd come back so soon, but glad, I think." She smiled, hating to be reminded that she was meant to be on leave, mourning her husband. Some people wouldn't understand why she'd returned so quickly, but they weren't her, didn't have to live in her skin, and they didn't know that Vinny would have given his blessing if he'd been here.

"Glad Kribbs didn't insist on you going home again. Purely selfish reasons. I doubt I could handle this case by myself." Mike slid his notebook into his shirt pocket — no suit jacket today; too hot again.

"Of course you could," she said, sad that he had no confidence in himself after all these years. "You'd have gone out there with Fran or Leona and just got on with it."

"I prefer being the silent partner, to be honest. You're better at getting info out of people. I'm better at writing it all down."

"I could say you're just lazy." She nudged him in the side. "But I won't."

"Lazy, me?" He grinned and stood. "I'll show you lazy. Last one down to the car buys lunch."

"Oh, get lost, you. I have no energy to race down the bloody stairs. Anyway, I bought lunch yesterday, remember, so it's your turn."

They said tarra to Fran and Leona, leaving them to get on with what they did best — poking about into dead people's lives and their families, plus checking CCTV to see if a white Transit cropped up in the early hours of the morning.

In the car, she drove down the road then turned left onto another, parking outside the tall glass-and-brick office block, the business address of the estate agent, a solicitor, a cleaning company, and God knew what else.

In reception, a security guard stood behind a white podium, complete with a buttoned-to-the-collar blue shirt, a tie, and a navy suit jacket, the word SECURITY on the tops of the arms. Bethany would have said he must be hot, but the place had air-conditioning, and it was pretty chilly.

He smiled. "Sign in, please."

She showed him her ID anyway, then jotted their names in a ledger on the podium.

"Someone in trouble, are they?" he asked, wiggling the knot of his tie as though gearing himself up to help them apprehend someone.

"Not as far as we're aware," she said then walked over to the wall where a large poster in a frame showed the layout of the various floors and where each company was. "First level," she said to Mike, who now stood beside her. "We can walk."

They took the stairs to the left and came out on a long, slim hallway, several doors on either side, each with opaque glass in the top and bearing the company logos. She found one for Shadwell Estate and wondered why they didn't have a shop in the city instead. More chance of grabbing people's attention that way, with pictures of houses in the window.

She opened the door, and a dark-skinned lady stood from behind a desk in a massive room with images of houses in transparent plastic stands dotted about the space. Everything was white, and it seemed like the pictures floated. Other people worked behind glass desks and didn't bother to look up to see who had entered.

"Can I help you?" the woman asked.

"We need to talk to Yazeem Thomas," Bethany said, holding up her ID.

"That's me. Has something happened at one of the houses we rent out?" She rested a hand on her chest over a cream silk blouse, her red nails standing out against it.

"Not unless you have eighty-four Bawden Avenue on your books . . ."

"Ellie White's place?" Yazeem frowned. "Yes, she rents from us."

"Is there somewhere we can talk in private?" Bethany glanced about, spotting a door to the right, hoping it wasn't a poky kitchenette or a broom cupboard. "What about in there?"

"That's my husband's office — we run this business. Hang on while I go and speak to him."

"Uh, we'll come with you." If this woman was involved in Ellie's death, Bethany didn't want her being able to speak to her husband about anything — like an alibi.

"Of course."

Yazeem led the way, the hem of her black pencil skirt reaching to just above her knees, and once they were all inside, she shut the door. This room was the opposite to the other — all black — and her husband sat staring at a computer monitor, engrossed in whatever it was he worked on.

"Wesley, can we have a moment, please?" Yazeem walked over to him.

He glanced up at her, smiling, his blond hair at odds with his light-brown hipster beard. "What is it, love?"

She glanced over at Bethany and Mike, then Wesley did, too.

"Oh, I do apologise. I didn't realise anyone else had come in," he said, rising and coming around to offer a handshake.

Bethany and Mike took turns in greeting him, then Yazeem pulled two folding chairs out of a cupboard and set them up beside the other one in front of the desk.

"Would you like to sit down?" she asked.

"Yes, that'd be lovely." Bethany rearranged the chairs so they were in a semicircle, not a straight line. She needed to be able to see everyone.

Wesley scooted around to his seat and got comfortable, balancing an ankle on his knee, propping his elbows on the chair arms. He steepled his fingers. "Which property are you interested in, Mr and Mrs . . . ?" He smiled, his salesman persona firmly in place.

Christ, that stung more than Bethany expected. There was no Mr to her Mrs anymore, and that fact burrowed away in her heart and threatened to bring on tears as well as pain.

She cleared her throat and blinked. "We're not married, we're partners."

Wes nodded. "Yes, that term is in use a lot these days, isn't it?"

"*Work* partners." Her ID made a reappearance. "DI Bethany Smith and DS Mike Wilkins. We're not here about a property as such, although you'll need to know about the one in Bawden Avenue, so . . ." Bethany paused. "First of all, I need to ask some questions about Ellie White."

"Is she all right?" Yazeem asked, crossing her legs at the ankles. Her shoes looked expensive. Faux snakeskin.

At least I bloody hope it's fake.

If Ellie's mates were all in some kind of friendship group, why hadn't Sunbeam let the others know what had happened? Wasn't that off?

"Have you not heard from Sunbeam?" Bethany asked.

Yazeem shook her head, then raised her eyebrows. "Actually, I haven't checked my personal phone since yesterday morning. *Should* I have heard from her?"

"I would have thought so. Not to worry. How do you get on with Ellie?"

"Oh, she's lovely. We're best friends." Yazeem smiled. "I haven't heard from her either, not since the day before yesterday. She was going on a date and wanted to borrow a dress."

The red one? Bethany's heart skipped a beat. "What sort?"

"It's black, but it was in the dry cleaner's, so I couldn't lend it to her. I think she said she'd wear a purple one of hers instead. It has a glitter effect all over it." Yazeem appeared uncomfortable. "Sorry, I have no idea why I told you that."

"It's fine." Bethany smiled, hoping it made the woman feel better. "Did she tell you who she was going out with — and where to?"

"Mezzo's, but as for the man, no. She said I wouldn't approve so it was best I was kept out of it until she saw if it was going anywhere."

"What do you think she meant by you not approving?" Bethany asked.

"It's probably someone I don't like. She's a kind-hearted person, and I'm sick of her seeing men who treat her badly."

"Do you have the names of her previous boyfriends?"

"Only from the one serious relationship she had, and he was David Flynn. She was with him from age eighteen to twenty-eight, and he was the only fella who was nice to her. The blokes she saw after that . . . pigs, the lot of them, and that's me putting it mildly."

"Why did she split up with David?"

"They grew apart, nothing more than that. Ellie's a homebody, and David likes going to pubs and having holidays abroad — he's a bit of a social butterfly. Ellie's more of a week-in-a-Weymouth-caravan kind of girl."

Butterfly . . . Could he be connected to this?

Mike scribbled in his notebook then looked Bethany's way, eyebrows raised.

"Would anyone like a cold drink?" Wesley got up and went to a small black wine fridge sitting on top of a three-drawer filing cabinet and took out bottles of strawberry-flavoured water. He handed them around.

"Thank you," Bethany said, opening hers and taking a sip. "Okay, do you know of anyone who has a grudge against Ellie?"

Yazeem laughed throatily. "God, no, unless you count the men on those dates. But she hasn't seen anyone for over a year, so I doubt they'd be upset with her by now, just because she didn't want to see them again."

You'd be surprised . . .

"How does everyone in your friendship group get on?" Bethany took another pull on her water. It was going down lovely.

Yazeem grimaced. "Simon and James don't rub along too well, but they never have. James tolerates him for the sake of the gang. I think, after a few bust-ups over the years, they've agreed to just grin and bear it."

"Why don't they get along?"

"James thinks Simon is a waster, and it sounds horrible, but so do I, especially in recent years. Simon isn't exactly nice to his ex-girlfriend, Natasha."

"Natasha who?"

"Vanton. She's got three kids with him, boys, and he'd rather drink, amongst other things, than be with them. She kicked him out a while ago, and he's intent on getting her back, but I don't think that's likely. James disagrees with the way Simon is with Natasha and the kids. He always says Simon ought to be with the children more. It upsets James because he never knew his father, and his mother died when he was young."

"What about your other friend, Gavin?"

"Oh, he's nice." Yazeem glanced at Wesley. "You two played golf together, didn't you."

Wesley nodded. "Gavin is a great bloke. Simon, not so much. He's . . . well, I don't want to be rude, but he looks like a tramp."

Yazeem scratched her temple. "That's only because his clothes are a bit dirty and he has no teeth."

"And Sunbeam?"

"Oh, she's a scream. The party girl. I love her to bits."

Bethany needed to steer the conversation back to Ellie. "How do your friends feel about Ellie?"

Yazeem blinked. "They all love her. She's kind of the mother of the group, the voice of reason. She's quiet and calm and helps us all when we have any problems. She has a knack of knowing what to do to solve things."

"So no one in your circle would have wanted to harm her?"

"God, no. Why?"

Bethany took a deep breath. "I'm very sorry to bring this news to you, but Ellie has been murdered."

"What?" Yazeem clutched her throat. "How? When?"

"The night before last. We don't know the cause of death, just that it's suspicious. She was found in her garden wearing a red bridesmaid dress. Do you know why she would have had that on?"

"Oh God, give me a moment, please." Yazeem leaned forward and hung her head over her knees.

Wesley rushed around his desk and crouched, rubbing her back. "Deep breath, love."

Yazeem sat upright. "I can't . . ." She burst out crying, her mascara immediately running. "Why would anyone want to kill her?"

"We've yet to establish that, I'm afraid." Bethany reached to Wesley's desk and pulled a tissue out of a fancy box. She handed it to Yazeem. "Does the dress ring any bells?"

"Absolutely not. Ellie would never wear anything like a bridesmaid dress to go out for a meal, and definitely not red. She doesn't like it, says it makes her feel tarty."

Yazeem cried again, her face in her hands, and Bethany drank more water until the woman had composed herself.

"I'm so sorry, Yaz," Wesley said. "I know how much you love her." He patted his wife's shoulder then glanced over at Bethany. "Can we leave this for now? Yaz has had a bit of a shock."

"Of course. Thank you for your time. You've been very helpful."

Bethany was glad to get out. They left the building, the heat seeming like the inside of an oven compared to the cool air indoors. They sat in the car with the windows open, staring through the windscreen.

"Your thoughts?" she asked.

Mike ran his hands over his face. "I doubt either of them have anything to do with it. I'm only guessing, though, going by their demeanours. Neither of them seemed closed off or cagey. Pretty open, the pair of them. Their body language was fine. No dodgy micro-expressions either."

"See, this is where you excel. You pick up on the minute things that I don't. What micro-expressions *did* you pick up?"

"A slight tic at the side of her eye when she spoke about Simon. Sounds like he's the one down on his luck. I wonder if they look at themselves now, all these years later, and find it hard to believe where they've all ended up." He opened his notebook. "Simon's on benefits, James is a property developer, Gavin is an IT whatever, Yazeem runs her own business, Sunbeam is a florist, and Ellie was a graphic artist. All of them have succeeded except for Simon. Would they have predicted that, even as kids?"

"I don't get where you're going with this." She frowned.

"Nowhere. Just musing."

"Who's next on our list?"

"Simon Knight. We ought to look into her ex as well. I'll ring Fran in a sec to get them on it."

"Come on then. Let's fit Simon in before lunch. And I'll have a Subway, thank you." She started the engine and grinned over at him. "Plus a cookie and a drink. Cheers."

He laughed and shook his head. "I don't know where you fit it all."

"In my greedy belly," she said, pulling out into traffic.

They laughed, and it felt wrong, disrespectful to Vinny, but then she imagined him smiling at her, encouraging her to enjoy life rather than dwell on his loss, and she laughed some more, welcoming how she felt.

CHAPTER SEVEN

Simon Knight's place was a scabby little effort, the front garden overgrown with long grass and weeds, thistles and dandelions in particular. The latter waggled their yellow or wispy, grey-white heads in the gentle breeze, their stems arched, as though they hadn't had enough water. The curtains were drawn at the two windows, one up, one down, and the front door had a blind behind the glass, which blocked out any view inside through the clear pane. Each property had an alleyway between them, most with wheelie bins backed against the walls.

Bethany knocked on the scarred front door, the green paint peeling in places, the original pale wood showing through. Weather scars. She knocked again and, after waiting a couple of minutes, decided they ought to check around the back. She led the way down the alley and accessed the garden via the tall slatted gate, which opened inwards to the left and blocked the view of the bottom half. Ahead was a patio, the closest end loaded with metal parts, perhaps the innards of washing machines, car engines, and random rods of steel.

"Looks like he's got a job on the side," Mike said. "Collecting and selling scrap."

"Hmm."

They stepped farther in, and Bethany closed the gate by reaching out behind her to push it to. The grass had to be close to knee height, and someone had walked through it from the edge of the patio to the rear of the garden, leaving a trodden line, the blades flat in that strip. Bethany skirted the metal mess and walked to the back door, knocking on it. She peered through the glass in the top into a kitchen that needed a jolly good clean. Takeaway boxes, Foster's cans, crisp packets, you name it, they were everywhere, on the worktops, the table, even on the four chairs. The floor had a good helping of them, too, and a little road had been created between it all from the external door to the internal.

"How the hell do people live like this?" she asked.

Mike came to stand beside her. He peered in. "Bloody hell! Fire hazard or what." He looked at Bethany. "I'm *so* sorry. That just popped out."

Although her eyes stung, she smiled. "No, it was good to hear it. Vinny would have said the same thing." She rapped on the glass again, swallowing the lump in her throat. "I suppose Knight could be anywhere if he's not tied down by a job."

Mike turned his back on the house and faced the garden. "Maybe he's gone to buy some black bags to clean up his grotty kitchen."

Bethany laughed.

Mike shoved his hands in his pockets. "I wonder why there's a path through the grass. I'll go and have a look. I'd say he was dumping rubbish down there, but that's highly unlikely, considering he seems to enjoy having it in his kitchen." He paused. "And if he was going down to the bottom of the garden, wouldn't the path be from where we are, not from the gate?"

Bethany turned to look. "Not necessarily. He could be storing something down there amongst the trees, and he brings it home via the gate and takes it straight there."

Mike stepped off the patio and formed his own path. Bethany followed. Unruly conifers spanned the end, so bushy their branches overlapped, creating complete privacy. The treetops went pretty high, and from where she stood, it seemed like they poked at the white, puffy clouds. Mike stopped short, and she bumped into him, her nose squashed against his shoulder. She took a step in reverse.

"Fuck," he said. "Go back to the patio."

"What's the matter?" Her heart clattered.

"There's a body."

"What?" She pulled her phone out of her pocket, turned, walked away, and accessed her contact list, her focus going straight to the name Rob Quarry, the front desk sergeant who worked the day shift. "How do you know they're dead?" she asked over her shoulder, going to stand by the door again.

"Because he has the same white makeup on as Ellie, including the weird blusher circles."

"Pardon?" She couldn't take it in. "Did you just say . . . ?"

Mike nodded. "I did." He went to the body.

Bethany shook, watching him.

"No pulse," he said.

Fuck. "I'll ring Rob, you do Isabelle. Then we'd better get out of this bloody garden."

They made their calls and then returned to the car. Rob was sending uniform to do house-to-house, and Isabelle and her team, plus Presley, were on the way.

Bethany took protective clothing out of the boot and handed a set to Mike. "We could have fucked up the scene." She bit her lip. "We tromped through that grass."

"I doubt we've done any damage. The bit we walked on hadn't been touched for ages. That's got to be about three or four months of growth there. You'd think he'd have been able to make a lawnmower out of all that metal and the engine, wouldn't you."

She smiled, despite the dour situation. "Pack it in."

"What? It made you grin, didn't it?"

"Yes, but—"

"Well, then, it was worth it."

They put the clothing on, Bethany cursing the hot weather. Having an extra layer would have her sweating in no time.

"We're not going to get that ruddy Subway for lunch, are we? Well, not for ages anyway," she said, her stomach making a ribald complaint, a rarity since Vinny had died. "I'm uneasy that two friends from the same group are now dead." She'd lowered her voice in case any neighbours heard her through their open windows.

"It's more than suss," he said. "Blimey, I'm not putting my hood up until I have to. It's too bloody hot."

She pulled hers down and undid the front zip. She'd do it up when they had to go back into the garden. While she waited out the front for the uniforms and SOCO, Mike took some crime scene tape down the alley and tied a strip to the circular gate handle.

"Stand guard by that gate, will you?" she called to him.

Bethany studied the area — all of the houses were decent apart from Simon Knight's. She wondered whether he rented from Yazeem and Wesley Thomas, too. If so, they weren't keeping up with checks and ensuring he was doing the gardening.

A young, skinny blond bloke came trotting along the street, the white wires from his headphones snaking from his ears and down beneath his red T-shirt. Sweat patches crept out from under his arms, and a triangle of dampness covered the chest. He walked as though to a beat, and she guessed it was something slow and steady from the way he loped. She smiled at him as he came closer, and he frowned, looking from her to Simon's house and back to her again, his face paling.

Then he turned tail and ran.

"Stop!" She legged it after him, her leg muscles upset at the sudden exercise.

He glanced behind him, and the action meant he tripped over his own feet, going flying down onto the pavement. "Oof! Fuck it."

"What the hell are you running for?" she said, coming to a stop beside him, out of breath and ashamed about it.

She'd only gone a few metres, so why the need to gasp? "Get up — and don't even think about scarpering again." Great. Her short spurt had her forehead sweating.

He scrambled to his feet and pulled the earbuds out, tinny music babbling from them. "W-what are you doing outside Simon's wearing that?" He pointed to her suit.

"I'm a police officer." She fished her ID out, keeping her attention on him in case he had a mind to have another go at sprinting.

He widened his eyes and backed away, hands up. "I'm off then. If he's in the shit, I don't want anything to do with it."

"Wait for a moment, please. My *male* colleague is just down there, and you don't want *him* chasing you. Just answer a few questions, then you can leave." *If I don't think you're involved in this.* "What's your name?"

"Aww, man, if I tell you, you'll think of some reason to nick me." He shuffled from foot to foot, clearly uneasy.

"Why would I do that? Have you got previous?"

He nodded and raked his hand through his mangy hair. Kicked at some loose stones on the pavement.

"What for?" she asked, although she had a good idea.

"Dealing." He'd said it like a sulky kid, quietly, his tone low, as if her not hearing him meant he hadn't said it.

"What are you selling?"

"Weed."

"Do you manufacture?" She held her breath.

"Fuck, no. I just deliver."

His response was too immediate and genuine for her to disbelieve him. "Are you carrying now?"

"No."

Thank God for that. "Then, quite frankly, between you and me, I don't give a toss, all right? What's your name?"

"Fuck's sake. You're not shitting me, are you?"

She shook her head. "I assure you, I have more important things on my plate than bothering about you." *Like a dead husband and two bodies.* "So please, just cooperate. I'm really not in the mood to stand here arguing. And if you're quick about it, you'll be on your way before a load of other coppers turn up, okay?"

He nodded and eyed her as though he didn't trust her one bit. "Zebedee."

She sighed. "Come on now. Do you think I was born yesterday? Stop fucking me about. I haven't got the patience."

"I'm serious. That's my name." He coloured up, obviously embarrassed by it.

She kind of felt sorry for him. "Surname?"

"You don't need it. All you've got to do is look me up on your files. You'll see me."

She couldn't be arsed to push for it. "How do you know Simon Knight, or is that a stupid question?"

"It's a stupid question." He gave her a sheepish grin.

She returned it. He was probably a good kid underneath it all and just sold weed because he either had to for the money or he'd been dragged into it by some gang. "Did he only get weed from you? What I mean by that is, did he buy anything else from you other than weed?"

"No, he only bought weed cos that's all I deal, and I already told you that. Are you trying to catch me out?"

"Believe me, mate, I haven't got the energy for that. Was he supposed to be buying from you today?"

"No, he owes me money for the last lot he had. That's why I'm here. Thirty quid. I can't let that go."

"I'm sure you can't. How long has he been buying from you?"

"About a year."

"You said you only distribute. Is it possible he could have pissed off whoever you get the gear from?"

"He might have, but it'd be news to me, and no, I'm not telling you who that is. Again, if you look up my file, you'll find out for yourself. If I'm caught blabbing, I'm in trouble, know what I mean?"

Unfortunately, she did. "I'm not here to get you in the shit. I just need information on Simon Knight. Look, if you know of anyone who might want to harm Simon, I need to know who it is."

"Harm him? In what way?" He stared at her.

Something must have shown on her face. He backed away.

"No, not that. People might want to deck him, but not that."

"Okay, thank you for your help." She spotted the SOCO van turning into the street behind him. "I'd go now if I were you. Keep your head down and your nose out of trouble, understand?"

He nodded and scooted off.

SOCO pulled in against the kerb and Isabelle jumped out. While she and her colleagues got their gear on, Bethany explained why she was there and what Mike had seen in the garden.

"Christ, what is this, serial killer month?" Isabelle rolled her eyes, lifting her hood.

Bethany did the same then drew up the zip, already feeling hotter. "Not a serial yet. You need three bodies for that."

"All right, smarty pants, spoil my joke why don't you. Which house?"

Bethany strode ahead and took the SOCO team down the alley. "In there, at the bottom."

"A bit of a theme then." Isabelle went into the garden.

Bethany waited until everyone else had followed, then she shut the gate and walked with Mike out onto the pavement. Uniforms had arrived.

"Ooh, get us," she said. "We've had three sent our way."

"Crikey." Mike yanked his hood off. "This heat is seriously getting my goat.

The uniforms approached — Glen Underby, Nicola Eccles, and Tory Yates.

"Hi, guys," Bethany said, then went on to explain the situation. "So the usual, please. I'd like one of you stationed outside the gate. We need a log setting up, so everyone already in the garden needs to sign it. They went in about two or three minutes ago."

"I'll do the gate," Tory said.

"Thought you would." Bethany smiled.

Tory looked awkward. "I'm sorry about Vi—"

"Don't," Mike said. "Beth wants to—"

"Thank you, Tory," Bethany said. "I'm not ready to speak about it yet, so we'll just continue as though it hasn't happened, all right? Now, you go to the gate — we'll be in there in a sec ourselves — and you, Glen and Nicola, do your thing with the neighbours. If any of them mention a Zebedee, I'm aware of him."

"Zebedee Hollingworth?" Glen asked.

She nodded. "I expect so. Dope dealer."

"Yes, that's him."

"Well, like I said, I'm aware of him, but if they have any info on him other than that he sells the victim weed, then I'll need to know. So, as far as we're aware, the deceased is a Simon Knight, although we haven't seen any identification as of yet, so it could be anyone. I'm particularly interested in a white Transit, but don't mention it to the neighbours as it puts thoughts in their heads that might not really exist." She thought about Polly Dilway saying the Transit had been in Bawden Avenue for an hour during the day. "Ask them if anyone's been parked down here and stayed in a vehicle for any amount of time. Also, keep an eye out for home CCTV. If you see any cameras, ask if they're dummies. If any are real, request copies of recordings from the last forty-eight hours."

Glen and Nicola bobbed their heads.

"Okay, on you go. If we're gone by the time you've finished and you find anything out, just get hold of me by phone." She turned to Mike. "Come on, fella. Let's go and see what's going on with this poor sod down in the garden."

CHAPTER EIGHT

James stood in an empty house he was working on renovating, and the trill of his phone echoed, startling him out of his head and into the present. He'd been thinking of how he'd staged Simon in that overgrown jungle he'd called a garden.

He glanced at his screen: YAZEEM.

Bollocks. She'd probably heard about Ellie and wanted to tell him. Now he'd have to pretend he cared in order to keep up the charade. Wonderful. Still, he'd been expecting it — a lot sooner, to be honest. He'd been surprised she hadn't called him yesterday. He'd planned Ellie's murder so she'd be found on Sunbeam's day off, and with all the police presence, Sun was bound to have found out who had been killed, then she'd have spread the news. However, she hadn't — not that he was aware of anyway. She certainly hadn't rung him.

He swiped the screen and held the mobile to his ear. "Hi, lovely. How are you?" He wanted to be sick at how nice he'd sounded, as though he actually liked Yazeem. He had once upon a time, before they'd all ripped the piss out of him on that fateful night that had changed everything.

"James . . ." She sniffed. "I've got some terrible news."

Here we go. Dramatics are on the way. "What's the matter? Are you okay? Is Wes all right?" God, he was good at this. He almost laughed, but that wouldn't be the done thing, would it. No, he had to behave himself.

"I'm fine, so is Wes. You're so sweet for asking. But it's . . . it's our Ellie."

"God, did she have trouble from that man she was meeting for a date? If she did, I'll find out who he is and sort him out." *Haha. Hahahah.*

"She told you about it?"

"She did. Why wouldn't she?"

"Sorry, I'm not thinking straight. Of course she'd tell you things like that. We tell each other most things, don't we." She sniffed again.

The sound was getting on his wick.

"Did she tell you who she was meeting? The police want to know." She paused.

He filled the awkward silence. "No, she just said she had a date. I told her to be careful, because you just don't know with people these days, do you." *Big fat LOL.*

"No, you don't, and it seems he might have been a bad person, the man she met," she said. "I may as well just get it out there. Ellie . . . Ellie's been murdered."

"What?" he shouted, pleased at how he'd come across — shocked, upset. Someone who gave a shit. Hilarity bubbled up, and he squashed it down. "When?"

"The night before last, apparently — the night she went out with that bloody bloke. Why didn't she tell one of us who he was?"

Because I told her not to.

Yazeem went on, "She was dumped in her garden, can you believe that? She was outside all night by herself." The last few words came out as a weird squeak.

Why was Yazeem bothered about *that*? Ellie had been dead. It wasn't like Ellie knew where she was, for God's sake. Yazeem could be such a dumb cow sometimes.

"That's really sad," he said. "The poor thing. I just can't believe it. How was she killed?"

"I don't know."

I do. "How did you find out?"

Sun must have told her, that had to be it. He was naffed off she hadn't phoned him as well, though. Typical. They were all meant to be mates, had promised to stick together, and there he was, left out of the loop.

"The police came to see me at work," she said.

What the . . . ?

"I expect they'll want to talk to you lot as well," she went on. "They asked about you."

Me specifically? Why? Did I cock up somewhere? "Did they? What for?"

"Oh, the detective, can't remember her name, wanted to know how we all got along. I said it was fine apart from you and Simon."

You stupid fucking bitch. What were you playing at? "What did you say that for?"

"I wasn't going to lie to a copper!"

"What did you tell her?"

"Just that you two have never really got along but have agreed to behave yourselves. What's wrong with that?"

"Nothing." But there was something wrong with it. Now they might suspect him of murdering Simon. *I should have left him until last and let him take the blame for killing everyone.*

"Are you still there, J?"

"Yep, just trying to take it all in. I can't get over the fact she's gone." He also couldn't believe the police might be on to him quicker than he'd anticipated. He'd planned to kill them all then bugger off abroad. He had a fake passport in a new name and enough money to survive for the rest of his life if he lived frugally, although he'd start his business up wherever he landed. He had too much know-how regarding property development to let it go to waste — and there was more cash to be earned.

"It's awful, isn't it?" Yazeem said, sniffing yet again.

He gritted his teeth and imagined punching her face in.

Yazeem sighed. "I spoke to Sun. I was surprised she hadn't rung me, to be honest, but she said she was so upset she went inside herself and couldn't face talking to any of us. Her neighbour was the one to suggest phoning the police. Sun was on her way to check on Ellie, because she'd seen her in the garden from her bedroom window, but the neighbour stopped her. She mentioned a white Transit backing up to Ellie's on the night of the murder. Oh God, what if her body was in the back? I hadn't thought of that until now."

"Oh dear." He'd said that more for himself than her. He hadn't expected anyone to have seen the van. It had been three in the bloody morning. Who the hell looked out of their windows at that time?

"Who saw it?" he asked.

"That old lady, Polly Dilway. You know the one. Ellie got some shopping for her if her legs were playing her up."

He knew exactly who she meant. Ellie was always banging on about the old girl.

"And whoever did this to Ellie put her in a red dress," Yazeem all but shrieked. "She *hated* red, didn't she?"

He bit his lip to stop himself from giggling. "Yes, she hated red. How awful. She'll be turning in her grave." He hadn't been able to resist that little joke.

"James! For God's sake! Do you have to?"

"Sorry, it popped out. Should we all meet, raise a glass to her or something?" That was the last thing he wanted to do, spending more time with his so-called friends unless it was their kill night, but it was what she'd expect him to say, and it was best he stuck to his usual responses, the kind and caring buddy.

"I think we should. It's only right," Yazeem said.

"Okay, what about tomorrow lunchtime?" He was knackered and needed a good night's sleep so wouldn't be drowning anyone tonight, but then again, in light of what Yazeem had told him about Ellie's neighbour, he had something to rectify. He hadn't expected a deviation in the plan, but he'd deal with it regardless.

"That's fine. Shall we meet in the usual place?" she asked.

"Yes, that's what Ellie would have wanted. Have you told the others yet?"

"I tried Simon, but he's not picking up. I expect he's smashed off his face. And Gavin was devastated."

So she'd left James until last. Why wasn't he surprised? "Okay, well, let the others know we're meeting up at one o'clock, and I'll spring for the drinks and a spot of lunch."

"You're so good to us," she said.

He pinched his nose to stop himself from laughing yet again. He'd be anything *but* good to them soon. "See you then."

He slid his phone away, the mirth instantly fading, hurt that everyone else had been called before him. He'd always known he wasn't as close to Yazeem as some of the others, but he'd thought she liked him more than Gavin or Simon.

Mania came knocking, rumbling inside him, and James let the persistent laughter out. Yazeem thinking Simon was off his head on booze or weed was one of the funniest things ever, considering what James had done to him. She'd soon find out exactly where Simon was, and she'd probably let James know last then as well.

Still, after he'd sorted that Polly woman, Yazeem was next after she'd been to yoga tomorrow night. There was the potential to get an apology out of her, although she'd cracked up when he'd told her about his childhood, just like all the others, so if she found it funny, would she be the same as Ellie and Simon and refuse to say sorry?

Time would tell.

CHAPTER NINE

With the scene photographed as well as the body, Bethany, Mike, and Isabelle moved to stand around the corpse.

The weird game mouthpiece was in place, revealing gums and only one rotten tooth, plus half a tongue. It didn't appear as though the other teeth had been removed as there were no holes or blood. The gums had healed at some point in the past.

"What's with that freaky makeup?" Isabelle said. "And a moustache has been drawn with what looks like kohl liner — if you can call that a moustache. Looks more like a line to me. Why the blue eyeshadow? It's definitely got to mean something. Ellie had similar." She frowned, bending over to peer closer. "He has weird eyelashes, too, although they're not quite the same as Ellie's. They seem thinner."

Bethany had a look — without bending too close. "I agree. They're fake. He has a plug in his ear as well."

"In both," Mike said from the other side of the body. "So there'll be things in them, no doubt."

"I wonder why there's the bug theme? And the garden as a resting place?" Bethany used the heel of her hand to scratch her head. All this creepy-crawly talk had her itching, same as it had at Ellie's scene.

"It'll come clear at some point, I imagine," Isabelle said. "Nice suit, and I like that red tie." She pointed at the victim.

"Ellie had a posh red dress, he's in a suit. Red tie. Possibly significant?" Mike said.

"Probably." Bethany stared at the dead man.

A white shirt, which looked as though it had been ironed. A blue suit. If this was Simon Knight, the attire didn't match the description Yazeem Thomas had given. Hadn't she mentioned dirty clothes? Wesley had said Simon was like a tramp. The cheeks had the same circles of blusher on them, and dandelion leaves had been stuffed up his nostrils. Bethany thought of the dope he'd bought off Zebedee and betted Simon hadn't expected to have *those* sorts of weeds in his possession, the type he couldn't smoke and get high on.

A large, hairy spider peered out from beneath the suit jacket lapel, and Bethany squealed, jumping back. It looked stark against the white shirt, and she shivered. "Christ, what the hell is *wrong* with this killer?"

Isabelle scooped the little fucker up into an evidence tub and slapped on the lid as though it was nothing.

"Ugh. It could have crawled on you if you weren't quick enough." Bethany reared away, the spider scrabbling about inside in an attempt to get out. Vinny had always dealt with the spiders at home. Now she'd have to catch them herself.

He entered her head at random times. Why does grief follow you in your day-to-day life, even when you are busy, and catch you unawares with its evil intensity? She took a deep breath and switched off her mind to try and stop thinking of him. It was all still too raw.

"They're more scared of us than we are of them." Isabelle smiled, lunging towards Bethany with the tub held out.

"Piss off," Bethany said and held a hand up. "I mean it. When it comes to spiders purposely being put under my nose, don't blame me if I punch you in the face."

Isabelle laughed and handed the tub off to a SOCO. "Sorry. I forget that some people are scared of them."

"Well, don't. It isn't funny." Bethany had the hump now and needed a moment to calm down, so she stared at the flower placed in Simon's hand — that was if it *was* Simon Knight. Yesterday, Fran had discovered the bloom was a gerbera, a kind of daisy. It definitely had to mean something to the killer for them to have been placed on both bodies. "Did you find any ID on him while we were out the front?"

Isabelle nodded. "Simon Knight."

"So it's him then. That makes it two people from the same friendship group that have been murdered." Bethany sighed, wondering whether there was something in their pasts that had led to this. She sent a message to Fran and asked her to find out the next of kin.

"Ay up, Elvis himself is here." Isabelle nodded behind Bethany.

Bethany pressed the Send button. "Don't let him hear you calling him that." She turned and smiled at Presley.

"Well, it's a good job it's sunny, that's all I can say because . . . no tent?" Presley asked, coming to stand by the body.

"The lads are sorting it now." Isabelle glanced at her watch. "Mind you, they've been gone ten minutes. I'll go and see what they're playing at. Feel free to touch the body, but don't move it yet. We've taken the pictures already, but we might need more." She walked off along the flattened path of grass.

Presley stared at Simon. "I wonder if he died the same way as Ellie."

"And how was that?" Bethany asked, seeing as he hadn't sent her an email about Ellie's PM yet.

"She drowned," Presley said.

"What?" Mike gaped.

Presley nodded. "Exactly what I said. A drowning. Water in the lungs et cetera, although none in her ears, which suggests to me just her face was placed in water."

Bethany frowned. "What, like in a sink or bath?"

"Yes, and hair is missing at the back, ripped out by the roots, so someone either yanked her about by it or gripped it tight while they held her head over the water — and the water has been sent to be analysed. She had a scent to her, and swabs have gone off to the lab to determine what that is as well. I think she was drowned then washed, then the makeup was applied. The hair was definitely shampooed and conditioned, then styled with a curling iron."

"That could have been done before she went out, though," Bethany said. "She was going on a date."

"I can't see someone being able to drown her and not get her hair wet, unless they were fugging weird and put one of those shower caps on her," Mike said.

"True." Bethany couldn't imagine how anyone could hold someone's face in water like that. "Wouldn't she have struggled? Was there anything under her fingernails where she tried to fight them off?"

"Again, off at the lab, although it doesn't look like skin to me. There's more." Presley grimaced. "I'd say she was brought back to life a couple of times. There's bruising on her nose where the nostrils had been pinched, among other signs, one of which being cracked ribs from CPR."

"You what? Someone drowned her then did CPR?" She blinked, unable to believe the degree of sickness this individual had in them. "Why would they *do* that?" She was musing to herself, not expecting anyone to reply. "Maybe they enjoyed toying with her, seeing her die, then watching her breathe again. A God-like power."

"Whatever, it's bloody gross, not to mention cruel." Mike shook his head, beads of sweat gathering just below the elasticated, bunched fabric of his hood on his brow. "Can you imagine her being relieved she was alive again, only to be drowned a second time? Or more? Fucking hell."

"I'll take the earbuds out, shall I?" Presley didn't wait for an answer. He knelt, drew his bag closer, and took out two plastic boxes, which he placed either side of the head beneath the ears.

As he had with Ellie, he used tweezers to remove one plug. Nothing scuttled out, much to Bethany's relief. He shone a torch in the ear.

"Ah, I see you." Presley inserted the tweezers and brought something out, holding it up and squinting. "Looks like a woodlouse all curled up in a ball." He popped the louse in an evidence tube then used the torch to look inside again. "There are a couple more in there by the looks of it." He replaced the plug then moved round to the other side, repeating the process. "I won't get this out. It can wait until I'm at the lab, but it appears to be a dead wasp."

Bethany shivered. She hated the damn things as much as spiders, maybe even a bit more. What did these insects *mean*? She was frustrated as hell and resisted stamping her foot. Her phone bleeped, saving her having a paddy, and she looked at the message.

Fran: SIMON'S PARENTS ARE DECEASED. NO OTHER FAMILY.

Well, that was just a big pile of crap.

Bethany: WHAT'S THE ADDRESS OF A NATASHA VANTON?

Fran: HANG ON.

While Bethany waited for a reply, she asked Presley, "Anything standing out to you?"

"No. It's the same as Ellie — no outward signs. His skin smells the same as Ellie's, and his suit has a chemical whiff. Dry cleaned?"

"That seems off with what we've been told about him — he apparently didn't dress too nicely; dirty clothes — plus his kitchen is a shit tip."

"They've clearly been dressed by the killer then." Presley rolled his eyes as though she was a bit dim.

It hurt her fragile feelings.

"I realise that. Ellie wouldn't have chosen a dress like that, especially not red, according to her friend, and Simon wouldn't wear what he's got on." Her message tone rang out, and she was relieved. Her temper was rising at Presley's remark, and this would stop her from biting his head off.

Fran: 41 ST JUDE COURT.

Bethany: THANKS.

"Mike, we have to go." She smiled at Presley — maybe she'd been oversensitive about what he'd said. Best she remove herself from the scene. "Before we go . . . anything in his mouth?" She hadn't let herself look, despite it gaping from the mouthpiece, dreading what she'd see.

He leaned over. "Another blue plastic butterfly. No tongue."

What the fuck?

SOCO came along with the tent, and she moved out of their way.

"Okay." She said goodbye and left the garden, signed the log, and removed her protective clothing. Then she waved at Tory and walked down the alley and into the street, Mike right behind her.

Isabelle stood at the kerb, talking to Nicola, who held her notebook out as if they were discussing what she'd written on it.

Bethany approached them. "Something going on?"

Nicola shook her head. "No one saw or heard anything, but a few people are out, so we'll have to come back later."

Bethany peered at Nicola's pad. It was a blank page. Perhaps she'd imagined them talking about her notes. Maybe grief made you paranoid as well as upset. "Okay. We're off to see the victim's ex-girlfriend, so if you hear something, get hold of me."

She got in the car, and just as Mike sat beside her, she had to take her phone out to read a message.

Leona: CCTV. WE'VE SPOTTED A VAN OUT ON BOTH NIGHTS, BUT THE CAMERAS ARE

ONLY IN SO MANY PLACES, SO WE HAVE TO GUESS WHERE THE VEHICLE WENT AFTER THAT. NO NUMBER PLATE — TOO DIRTY. WE'LL SORT A POSSIBLE AREA OF RESIDENCE ON THE MAP ASAP.

Bethany: OKAY, THANKS. WE'RE GOING TO SEE NATASHA VANTON AT 41 ST JUDE. WE'LL BE BACK AFTER THAT.

She pulled away, opening the windows. She needed a car with air-conditioning.

"I'm so hot it isn't funny," Mike said.

"Ego or what!"

She glanced over at him, and he frowned back. Then the penny dropped, and he laughed, fanning his face with his hand so she really knew why he'd said that. They chuckled on and off all the way to St Jude Court, which took the heaviness of today off her shoulders a little. Then, all too soon, she parked outside Natasha Vanton's, and the weight reappeared, sitting firmly on her shoulders as though it enjoyed living there and breathing down her neck.

"Let's get this over and done with," she said and got out of the car.

They stood at the front door, and Bethany pressed the bell. Kids' voices filtered out through a partly open window, plus the childish dialogue of some cartoon character or other.

A woman opened up, slim and blonde, about twenty-eight or so. She appeared tired and harassed, and Bethany supposed that with children, any woman might look the same way at times.

"Natasha Vanton?" Bethany produced her ID. "I'm DI Bethany Smith, and this is DS Mike Wilkins."

"Simon doesn't live here," she said, seeming pissed off, like she had visits from people looking for him all the time. "I've already told the police that, so why you keep coming round here, I don't know."

"Can we come in, love?" Bethany tilted her head at a small ginger boy of about eighteen months who'd appeared. He clung to his mother's leg, giving them a cheeky grin.

"What for? I told you, he doesn't live here. I don't have much to do with him anymore." Natasha sighed and stepped back, seeming to come to the conclusion that it was better to get this over and done with so she could carry on with her life. From what she'd said, it sounded as if Simon had been in trouble with the police before.

Fran would likely update them on that soon enough.

Natasha led them into a living room, where another lad, slightly older, sat watching something on a phone. An array of toys littered the floor, and the smaller child from the front door plonked himself on the rug and played with one of them.

"Do you want a drink?" Natasha asked, her expression saying she was too weary to make them one but would if she had to.

Bethany was thirsty, but she'd let the woman take a load off. "Have a seat. We're fine, thanks." She gauged the children to be too young to understand what she had to tell Natasha, otherwise she'd have advised they went into another room.

Natasha sat beside the older boy and ruffled his hair. "What's he done then?"

Bethany gave a wan smile. "When did you last see Simon?"

"Yesterday. He came here to see why I'd rung him."

"And why did you?"

Natasha stared as though she wanted to say: *What the fuck's that got to do with you?* Instead, she said, "I needed him to look after these two while I took my oldest to the dentist, but he didn't answer — which isn't unusual — so I sorted it myself. He nipped here, I told him why I'd needed him, he called me a slag and accused me of seeing a man called Bazza, whoever the hell that is, then he left."

"I see. What's your relationship like with Simon?"

"He's . . . not particularly pleasant. I think he has mental issues, but he won't see anyone about it. We've split up a few times, but this time is for good. I can't stand him. Anyway, why are you here? If he needs bail, you'll have to go and see his mates. They're all up each other's arses anyway, so I'm sure they'd club together and come up with the money. I'm skint so can't help him, and to be honest, I don't want to."

"Where were you after he left here yesterday?"

"I took Archie to the dentist — my friend looked after these two — then I had dinner at her house. We do that about once a week. I stayed there until about seven, walked home, then got the kids to bed. I logged on to work's database around eight and did some entries I didn't have time to do last Friday. I work part-time, so fitting it all in is a bit of a nightmare."

"Is the database live?"

"What, like can you see what time I logged stuff? Yes."

Bethany smiled. "What time did you finish?"

"After midnight."

A man appeared in the living room doorway, and Bethany shifted her eyebrows upwards. She hadn't realised anyone else was here.

"Sorry, I tried to stay out of the way, but I have to go," he said. "I popped here between jobs."

"And you are?" Bethany asked.

He stared at her, probably thinking she had no right to ask and was a nosy mare. "James Obbington."

"Ah, I need to talk to you," Bethany said. "So for the moment, you're not going anywhere."

CHAPTER TEN

So for the moment, you're not going anywhere.

The words echoed in James' mind. Fuck, fuck, fuck. He really didn't need this. He'd been eavesdropping in the kitchen and thought he could dip out without being asked who he was. No such luck. That woman copper, he could tell she was a clever bitch. He'd have to be careful. This was too close for comfort. He'd thought he had a bit more time before they came to question him. He should have known they'd come here after they'd discovered the body.

What had they thought of the weeds up Simon's nose? Such a nice touch.

"What do you need to speak to me for?" he asked her casually, his carefully crafted alibi sitting on his tongue, waiting to come out. He was ready. She wouldn't be able to trip him up.

"Where were you last night and the night before?" she asked.

She studied him, assessing, trying to get under his skin, he reckoned. The bloke stared, too, but he seemed kinder somehow, easier to manipulate. Bargain.

James addressed the man. "I actually stayed over in The Ringer Hotel. My bathroom at home had a leak overnight, and it soaked the floor quite a bit, so I have my builders sorting it out."

"Your builders?" the woman said.

What's her name? Bethany Smith?

"I own a property development company." He smiled. "Lucky for me, otherwise it would have cost me a fortune. I'm staying there tonight as well." He wasn't. What he'd done a couple of days ago was booked in, told them he was unwell and wasn't to be disturbed — "Dodgy tummy after eating some salmon at a work's meal, you know how it is . . ." — and waited for reception to be clear after being in his room for a while, then snuck out again. Maybe he ought to go there later after seeing to the Polly Dilway woman, give the hotel staff a refresher on his face in case these two plods went snooping, asking questions. "Room twenty-eight, in case you need to know. Why did I have to say where I was?"

The bloke — if James remembered right, he was called Wilkins — wrote in his notebook.

Smith nodded absently. Was she mulling the information over? Getting his measure? Seeing things he thought he could hide, things she'd been trained to spot?

Bollocks, that's not good.

"We heard you and Simon Knight didn't get along," she said, piercing him with those all-knowing eyes of hers.

Natasha didn't seem to pick up on Smith's past tense slip.

Smith looked a bit haggard, as though she'd had a shit life lately. She needed to stop eating a dinner or two an' all. Over a size fourteen. Not to his tastes.

He shrugged. "You can't like everyone, can you. He was a twat when we were kids and is a twat now. I mean, look, he's left Natasha here in the lurch, not giving her child support since he lost his job icing bloody biscuits." There was no point in him refuting what Yazeem had told them about his relationship with Simon. Better to be honest. To a degree.

He wanted to giggle.

"Now," Smith said, planting her feet farther apart. "Do either of you know of anyone who'd want to harm Ellie White?"

James got in there first. "Ellie? God, no."

Natasha frowned. "Why, has someone hit her or something?" She stroked her son's hair.

"What about Simon?" Smith asked, totally ignoring Natasha's question and glaring at James. "Do you know of anyone who might want to hurt him?"

Rude bitch. "Nope. I don't like him but wouldn't hurt him — well, apart from a punch or two when he gets on my nerves, but we've always had scraps. You're better off looking at that Zebedee bloke, his weed dealer." He turned to Natasha for authenticity reasons, to make him look like a top bloke. "He's been round here a few times, hasn't he, demanding money? Maybe he finally beat Simon up."

Natasha nodded. "I told him to piss off or I'd ring the police. People just don't get that Simon doesn't live here anymore — and he never will."

Ooh, that could be taken the wrong way, as if she'd killed him, but James didn't want her accused of that. "I don't blame you. Enough is enough. By the way, do you need any money? For nappies or whatever? That's why I came round."

She shook her head. "I'll manage. Thanks anyway. It's not like I haven't had to before, is it."

He'd only mentioned her needing cash so it gave him a genuine reason to be there in the eyes of the coppers.

Natasha sighed. "Has something happened to him or what? Lots of weird questions here."

Smith cleared her throat. "I'm sorry to have to tell you, but Ellie was found dead yesterday, and Simon this morning, in their back gardens."

James' skin went cold with just the mention of a garden. He came over all funny, which he hadn't expected — the past was still in his psyche — and he teetered.

"Are you all right, sir?" Smith asked, moving to put a hand on his elbow.

"Christ, what a shock. I just need to sit down a minute." He flopped onto one of the chairs.

Natasha hadn't said anything, just stared at Smith like she hadn't heard her right.

"Are you okay, Natasha?" Smith asked.

"Um . . .yes?"

"Can you stay here for a bit, Mr Obbington?" Smith cocked her head at him. "Or should I call someone else to come and sit with you?" she asked Natasha.

"I'll stay," James said, shaking his head like this was all news to him and it had taken his breath away, even though he was perfectly fine. *Simon's breath had been taken away a couple times.* He stifled a chuckle.

"How . . . ?" Natasha stared at her youngest on the rug.

"We're not sure yet regarding Simon, but Ellie was drowned." Smith smiled, maybe to appear sympathetic.

"Drowned?" Natasha flicked her head from side to side. "As for Simon, I bet he moved on to harder drugs and bloody overdosed." She was clearly disgusted instead of upset.

Was that because of how Simon had treated her? Was she so emotionless about him because he'd drained out whatever feelings she'd had for him, leaving her feeling nothing?

Smith glanced at her colleague. "We need to get going. Sorry to have brought you such sad news."

They left, closing the front door quietly behind them.

James breathed a sigh of relief.

Natasha laughed, a tad hysterically, and James wasn't sure what to do with her. It appeared she'd lost the plot.

"What's so funny?" he asked, perplexed, wanting to laugh, too.

"I only wished him dead yesterday," she said, cracking up some more, her head thrown back.

Her two sons giggled, the one on the floor clapping.

"You have no idea how much I hate him, and now he's gone." She all but wet herself, laughter spilling out of her, and she clutched her belly.

Simon must have been a worse wanker than James had thought if this was Natasha's reaction. How would her oldest boy take it? Archie? He hated Simon; they'd never got along. James could understand why.

"What the hell did he actually do to you?" he asked.

"You don't want to know, but fuck, I'm glad he's dead."

The laughter turned to tears then, maybe of joy, maybe some sorrow for the man Simon used to be, perhaps from relief, and James felt like he'd done her a service. He'd rid her of the scum in her life, and now she could move on, free of that little prick.

She cried for ages and, finally uncomfortable with it, James stood.

"I need to go, sorry," he said.

She got up and wiped her face, seeming to shove her emotions in a box somewhere inside herself, doing her best to smile and return to the no-nonsense attitude she'd adopted of late. He couldn't blame her for that. Simon had dragged her right down from the vibrant girl she'd been to a shell of her former self. James didn't think *she* even recognised who she was anymore because she'd changed so much.

Maybe he ought to stick around Shadwell for a bit, try to get her smiling again.

No. That wouldn't work. He needed to make himself scarce once he'd finished the gang off.

"There's five grand in your bread bin." He smiled at her, hoping she'd smile back so he'd know she'd be all right.

"What?" Her eyes widened, and she let out a nervous titter, like she thought he was messing her about. She appeared as though she was suspicious of him, giving her cash like that.

"I'm serious. And don't go using it to pay towards his funeral either. It's for you and the kids. Treat yourself. Be happy again."

He walked out before she could protest or displayed gratitude. He couldn't handle that. Simon deserved a pauper's grave. Hopefully, if Natasha stayed strong and kept the cash, that was what he'd get, a shitty cardboard box as a coffin and a cheapo cremation, no one there to see him off to Hell, the place he deserved to be.

At his car — thank God he hadn't driven the Transit here or those two coppers would have spotted it — he pulled down the window shade beside him, same as he had in the van, slapped on one of those sticky fake beards, some bushy brown eyebrows, and crammed his baseball cap in place. With black-framed specs on that had a massive plastic nose attached, he drove to Ellie's street and parked right outside that old lady's place, put gloves on, then got out, pleased to note the filth on his number plates hadn't worn off. He was glad he'd thought to do it on both vehicles.

The police must have packed up and gone from Ellie's. No copper stood outside her front door or in the mouth of her alley.

Bonus.

He strode down the side of Polly's and entered her garden, then tried her back door. As luck would have it, it was unlocked, so he stepped inside and crept through the kitchen and hallway, entering the living room.

The ancient biddy was asleep in her chair, mouth open, catching flies.

He shuddered at that, at the memories that tried to invade his mind, the sound of bluebottles buzzing filling his ears.

Anger stirred.

This would be easy. Too easy. He grabbed a pillow off her sagging sofa and approached her, placing it over her face.

Pushed.

Held it there while she struggled.

And only lifted it once she'd been still for a good couple of minutes.

Sorted. Job done.

In her back garden, he plucked a daisy from the grass and took it inside, resting it on the old gal's chest. In the absence of a gerbera, it would have to do. He spotted a lipstick on one of her cluttered cabinets and drew perfect circles on her cheeks, another clown to add to his collection. Shame he hadn't thought to bring the eyelashes and the mouthpiece, but time was of the essence here — it was still daylight, and anyone could spot him. The least amount of time he spent here the better. With a couple of things utilised from her stash of knickknacks, and a good root around in her bedroom and bathroom, producing well funny clues that had him laughing, he then strode out, back to his car, and drove home, only taking his disguise off once he'd pulled into the garage beside the Transit and shut the door.

Later, he'd go and stay at the hotel for the night.

Ah, that little jaunt to Ellie's neighbour had gone so smoothly.

Killing didn't get much easier than that.

* * *

The sound of the flies buzzing was a massive hum, even outside the shed, rising in a crescendo then falling, only to rise once again. It seemed worse because of the darkness. He shivered, and Auntie Angelica's hands on his shoulders seemed too heavy, like they'd push him down into the ground where she wanted him to be. She'd said that once: You belong in Hell, you little scrote.

He didn't know what a scrote was, but he'd bet it wasn't nice.

"Your friends are waiting for you," she said. "Can you hear them?"

Yes, he heard them all right, and imagined there being so many of them, more than he could count. He remembered the maggots. If there was one fly to every maggot, then he reckoned there'd be thousands of flies.

"Bluebottles", she'd told him. "They'll have big, fat, shiny bodies by now," she'd said. "And they have a green-blue tint, just like the beetles.

She took her hands off him and opened the padlock. He braced himself for the flies to come barrelling out at him and kept his mouth shut so they didn't find their way inside. He closed his eyes, trying not to pee himself.

The door creaked as it always did — Auntie must have opened it — and he held his breath. Nothing came out of the shed, but the flies grew louder, almost deafening as his fear factor crept up and exacerbated the noise. His terror fed on the incessant buzzing, weakening his knees and snapping his eyes open.

Auntie must have been in here before the maggots had changed into those pupa things she'd informed him about. A square of opaque netting had been attached to the walls, ceiling, and floor halfway in, keeping the flies inside. He almost cried with relief that he'd be on the clear side, where no creatures could touch him. The only thing was, Pretty Princess was in the back half, and for him to get through this torture, he'd need to hear her tune and imagine her dancing.

"Get in," Auntie Angelica said, giving him her usual shove in the back.

He obeyed, and she followed him, closing the door behind them.

"You're going to have such fun," she said, bending to turn on the large torch she must have put in the corner at some other time. She moved to the left-hand side and took hold of a rope attached to the net, then backed up to the door. "When I pull this, they'll all come out to meet you."

He shuddered, clenching so he didn't wee, and turned to watch her as she stepped into the garden then pushed the door to, just enough for the width of the rope to fit in the gap.

"Goodnight, you little twat."

What? He was spending the whole night in here?

She yanked the rope, and the netting came down, covering him in its ghostly grasp. He cried out, the noise of the flies even louder now, as though they spoke to each other, excited at having more space in which to fly. James fought the net, scrabbling until he managed to throw it off him, then instantly regretted it. He should have stayed hidden under it, then the flies couldn't get to him. Auntie had left the torch on, and the swarm created a blanket of humming black life, the flies so tightly packed he couldn't even make out the shed walls.

Urine trickled, and he flung himself down on the floor, crawling in the direction of where he thought Pretty Princess was in her box. He reached out, patting, patting some more, and finally his fingers came into contact with it. Winding it up, he then opened the lid, but the melody was barely audible amidst so much buzzing. He snatched at the net and dragged it towards him, covering him and Princess, some flies inevitably making it beneath with him.

He cried silently, shivering, straining his ears to pick up the beautiful tune. His life was a circus, and he was a caged creature, unable to break free.

Bring on the Clowns.

CHAPTER ELEVEN

Bethany had tossed and turned again all night. She'd been unsettled by Natasha's blank reaction to Simon dying. Had the man been that much of a waste of space that he'd stripped all feeling from his ex? At least she wouldn't have to suffer with grief like Bethany, and that was something. She wouldn't wish this on anyone.

A lonely bed. A lonely house. Lonely heart. Lonely every damn thing. It was tearing her apart when she thought about it, so she tried not to, but it was hard. Grief. It lived with you. Always there. Lurking. Ready to come out and grab you when you least expected it, when you thought it had gone into hiding, then there it was, peeking around the curtain you'd drawn across to hide the mourning, saying, "I'm still here . . ."

It would always be here.

She shoved some bread in the toaster — one slice, she couldn't face any more than that first thing. With her cup of coffee, she sat at the table, still unable to come to terms with the fact that Vinny wouldn't get up out of bed, the floorboards then the stairs creaking to let her know he'd smelt the toast and was on his way down to nick her slice, grinning. He'd have added Marmite on top of the butter, laughing at her groan of disgust, then chased her around the kitchen, trying to get her to have a taste.

"How can you say you don't like it when you haven't tried it?" he'd say.

"Fuck off!" was what he'd get back, then they'd kiss between giggles.

Tears stung her eyes, and she rested her forehead on the table and wept.

The toast popped. She ignored it.

Her coffee went cold. She ignored that, too.

Spent, she pushed herself to standing, her whole body heavy, and it seemed she'd been like that since he'd died, like love made you lighter, and when it was gone, it dragged you down. But she still had the love, and one day she'd remember it, not just in snippets that broke her, but big swaths of it, letting it envelop her in its kindness and remembrance of the past. At some point she'd smile and not cry.

Just not today. Or tomorrow.

She didn't bother eating the toast and downed the cold coffee, then grabbed her things and left the house, left the memories inside it that seemed to seep out of the walls every time she went inside.

She might have to move. It was too painful to stay.

In the car, she used a wet wipe from the glove box to wash her face and peeked at herself in the rearview mirror.

What a dog.

Taking a deep breath and slipping back into detective mode, she drove round to Mike's and beeped him at the kerb. He came out, frowning, and she turned her face to him when he sat beside her.

"A bad night?" he asked, lowering his hand so she could look away.

"A bad morning, too." She attempted a smile and failed. "Still . . ."

"If you want to talk . . ."

"I know." She inhaled, and it shuddered in her chest from where she'd been crying. "Thanks. I couldn't do this without you." And she couldn't.

She drove to the station, and they entered the building, Rob already behind the front desk sorting some bloke out so he could go home after a night in the cells. He raised his hand, motioning for them to wait, and she inwardly sighed.

"Go on up, if you like," she said to Mike.

He did, and she rested her back against the wall, waiting for Rob to finish explaining to the man that he couldn't leave the country and had to report to the station every day by ten a.m.

She thought about the work they'd done yesterday after seeing Gavin Yates, who hadn't had much to add to what she already knew from the other members of the friendship group — Simon and James didn't get on, Ellie was lovely.

They'd returned to the station and talked everything through with Fran and Leona, hashing things out, trying to come up with a reason someone would want to kill Ellie and Simon. Leona suggested someone from their pasts might have a motive, so today they'd be going through all their friends and family again to determine whether anyone lurked there who had the potential to kill. Along with speaking to David, Fran had found out who all of Ellie's other exes were. They had watertight alibis so were off the hook.

Had Simon been the man Ellie had planned to meet for the date? Maybe that was why she hadn't told the others who it was — they'd probably put her off, seeing as Simon was a bit of a loser. No, that couldn't be right; otherwise, why was Simon dead if he'd killed her the night before? Unless he'd staged his own death, put all those bugs on himself, and overdosed or something, then off he went to lay himself down in the garden.

Or was it one of the others? Yazeem, James, and Gavin had all seemed nice people, genuine, nothing to be suspicious of. Wesley had also seemed nice, as had Sunbeam and her friend, Carly. Still, it wouldn't hurt to suspect them all anyway. One of them could be an excellent actor.

The man being released walked out of the station and fist-bumped the air, and a woman came running across the car park, giving him a tackle-hug. It was scenes like these that had Bethany wondering why people committed crimes if they were so relieved after they'd been let go — and they had family worried and waiting for them. Why put them through that?

She pushed off the wall and walked to the front desk, leaning her elbows on it.

Rob grabbed a Post-it pad and ripped off the top page. He handed it to her. "A Sunbeam Drayton rang, said she'd only speak to you."

"What time was that?"

"Fifteen minutes before you got in. Ursula gave me the details when I switched shifts with her."

"Did she say what she wanted?"

"Something about a neighbour not answering the door." He tapped a few letters on his keyboard. "A Polly Dilway."

Bethany's stomach rolled over. She stared at the note, which had a phone number on it. "Okay, I'll give her a ring now." She made her way through a door into a hallway. The interview rooms were all empty, so she went inside the soft one and dialled Sunbeam, who answered right away.

"Hello? Who's that?" Sunbeam asked, her voice shaky.

"DI Bethany Smith. What's up?" She sat on one of the sofas. Her belly growled, moaning about being empty, yet she had no appetite.

"It's about Polly. Miss Dilway, the old girl who saw the Transit. Well, I went round there first thing to check if she wanted me to nip to Tesco after work to get her some bits and bobs — this is the day Ellie would normally have done it, only she can't, because . . . Anyway, Polly wouldn't answer the door, and I peeked through her nets in the living room window, and she's in her chair. She doesn't seem right."

Bethany's heart skipped a beat. "How so?"

"Like, she's asleep but not. I can't explain it."

Asleep but not? "Try to. What's off about it? Think."

"She actually looks dead. There, I've said it. But she can't be. She's just asleep."

"What do you mean by her looking dead?"

"She's all pale except for two red circles on her cheeks, and I'm sure she's got blue round her mouth."

Fuck it. "Okay, are you still there, at her place?"

"No, I'm at mine. I'm meant to be at work."

"Do you have a key for Polly's?"

"No, just Ellie's."

Shit. "Okay, stay put. I need to talk to you when I get there, so you'll have to go in to work later."

"That's fine. I own the shop. My employee can open up. I'll give her a quick ring. Do you think Polly *is* dead?"

How do I bloody know until I get there? Then again, the mention of red circles on her cheeks . . . Had she been murdered because the killer knew she'd spotted the Transit? "Like I said, stay put. We'll be there in ten minutes."

She cut the call and turned to Rob. "I need an ambulance and uniforms at . . . God, let me think . . . eighty-seven Bawden Avenue." She rang Mike upstairs. "Sorry, mate, but we need to get out on the road. Hurry up."

It seemed no sooner had she pocketed her phone and made for the front exit than Mike appeared with to-go cups of coffee and a small cardboard tray with blueberry muffins in it. She thanked the heavens for the food and rushed to the car, getting in. Mike handed her a muffin once she drove away, and she managed not only to eat it all before they arrived, but also tell Mike between bites what was going on.

Parking outside Polly's, she said, "Let's hope she's just asleep."

"She could have died from natural causes, you know. She is old."

"I realise that, but she's also got red circles on her cheeks. I forgot to mention that."

"Oh God . . ."

"I know. Where did you get the muffins from, by the way?"

"It's Fran's birthday."

"Bollocks. We need to stop off somewhere before we go back and get her some flowers and a card."

"Good. I said you had a surprise for her later from us two. I felt a right prat for forgetting."

"Nice save. Come on," — she switched to a Welsh accent — "let's see what's occurrin'."

They laughed — they both loved watching *Gavin and Stacey*.

Vinny had loved it, too.

Stop it. Just stop.

She got out of the car, letting out a long breath. "You may as well stay there for a minute and drink your coffee until I know what's what."

Bethany headed straight for Polly's living room window. Peering inside told her all she needed to know. It was clear the woman was dead, and from what was on her chest, their killer had struck yet again. She called in to cancel the ambulance and asked Rob to get hold of Isabelle and Presley.

Nicola and Tory got out of a police vehicle up the road a bit, and Bethany waited for them. Mike left the car and stood with them on the pavement.

"Okay, looks like a deceased resident in eighty-seven — it's likely murder, same killer as for Ellie White and Simon Knight," Bethany said. "If you two can begin doing house-to-house, that'd be great. Mike, we'll see if Polly's back door is open. If it is, then that could be the killer's entry and exit point."

She left the uniforms to it and took protective clothing, gloves, and booties out of the car. They dressed and then went down the alley beside Polly's. He entered the garden first, gave it the all clear, then they moved towards the house. No one had been laid out on the pristine lawn, thank goodness — but why hadn't Polly been placed there like the others?

"Door's open," Mike said. "No sign of forced entry."

"Either a lock pick or it was already open. Polly could have forgotten to secure it last night."

"Or it was daytime. She might have left it unlocked. Someone came in, killed her, then left, not putting her in the garden because it was still light out."

"And if that's not the scenario, and it was dark, why not put her in the garden?"

"She's been killed because of the Transit and not for the reason the others have been offed?"

"That's my thought, too. Inside now. People could be listening." She was also conscious of them wasting time if Polly *wasn't* dead. Dilly-dallying out here wasn't good — or protocol.

They stepped in, and Bethany followed him through to the living room. Polly sat in her chair, definitely dead, but Mike checked for a pulse just the same.

"Poor sod," he said.

She shook her head. "All this because she saw the van — so someone *knows* she saw it. Sunbeam did, but what about the others?"

"Depends on whether they've spoken to each other and discussed it all." Mike turned away from Polly to browse the stuffed cabinets. "I thought so . . ."

"Thought what?"

He faced Polly again. "She's got a piece of folded card in her mouth."

Bethany had seen it but hadn't wanted to acknowledge it. She looked down, bending over the body. "That's a postcard. You can see the address on the back, and there's a stamp." Shit, they'd have to wait until SOCO got there to know what picture was on it.

"Seems to me the postcard was just here." He pointed at one of the shelves. "And it hadn't been folded until it was put in her mouth. See the slim line in the dust?" He pointed again.

Yes, there was a line, but also a small circle. "So what's that then?" She gestured to it then studied the shelf above. A lipstick stood beside a photo of a smiling young couple. "They've used that on her bloody cheeks! The top and bottom of it is the same size as the clean circle in the dust."

"Hmm. That daisy on her chest probably came from her garden, and as for that *thing* on her chest. What is it?"

Bethany studied it. An ornament. Small. A scarab beetle or something. It looked like it had come out of a Kinder egg, except it was clearly not plastic and had cost a fair bit if the gold legs were real. Either way, it was an insect. "Whoever did this is letting us know it was them. No eyelashes, ear-plugs, missing tongue, or mouthpiece this time, though."

"That could mean this was an off-the-cuff murder, but they've left enough here to get their point across, as in: *Look, it's me again*. Bold bastard. They're laughing at us."

"Maybe." She peered at the shelves again. The beetle had been on the bottom one — the shape of its body and legs were clean patches in the dust. It was going to be one hell of a job for SOCO dusting all the crap Polly had collected. Hopefully they'd get a print that could help them.

A knock clattered on the front door, and Bethany went to open it. Isabelle stood there, her face clouded with an expression of sorrow.

"Is she gone?" she asked, stepping inside and moving out of the way so her team could troop in.

"Afraid so."

"Shit. See, this is why I don't like talking to people like I did to her. I prefer to be at the scene and leave that sort of thing to you. I liked her — she reminded me of my gran — and now she's bloody dead."

"It's all very sad."

"Any further forward?" Isabelle asked. "I mean, it's not like I have blood spatter pictures or anything like that to sit and go through with you so we could work out what happened. The scenes have been pretty clean. The killer carried them to their gardens, placed them down, then left. No footprints either, which is annoying."

"No, we're clutching at straws. Everyone in the friendship group seems nice. We've spoken to them all, plus Simon Knight's ex and—" Her email alert went off. She took her phone out to access it, then Presley walked in.

"That'll be from me," he said, giving her a sheepish grin. "I had it sitting in my draft folder all night. Was meant to have sent it before I clocked off yesterday. Sorry."

"You may as well just tell me what it is," she said, sliding her mobile away.

"It's to do with Simon. He had a whack to the back of the head before death, so maybe he fell or was pushed onto something. Whatever, it was quite a wallop. He also had hair ripped out and was drowned. He had a cracked rib."

"What kind of sicko are we dealing with here? And I'm wondering now whether the method of murder is saying something." Bethany closed her eyes briefly. Too much spun around in her mind. Questions, information, and Vinny telling her to catch the bastard. Did Polly look like the old lady Vinny hadn't been able to save? The one he'd got depressed about just before he'd died?

Mike blew out a breath, his cheeks inflating. "We should really get round and see Sunbeam."

"Hmm. We'll go now, then pop back here afterwards."

Presley might discover something that would help them catch a damn break.

They took their white suits and whatnot off and left them beside the door for when they came back. A SOCO came past to go up the stairs, and she supposed all of Polly's things would be photographed and dusted for prints. No one expected to leave this world as a victim of a crime.

Sadly, in this day and age, it happened all too frequently.

Out on the path, she took a moment to breathe, to still her mind, because her next thought prior to coming out had been: *And no one expects to have to live their life without the one they love in it.*

A dangerous thought. One that would have her crying inside a second if she entertained it further.

Damn grief.

CHAPTER TWELVE

"Get the foot spa, twat face." Auntie Angelica pointed at him, her fat finger wobbling.

He had to do this every Friday night. She said her feet ached after a long week standing behind the cheese counter in Tesco, serving 'rude bastards', and having her feet relaxed would set her up for a good weekend.

James was eleven, and he knew what it was like to have sore feet. It happened every time he stood in the garden for hours on end.

He scuttled into the kitchen and pulled the spa out of a cupboard. It was easy to carry it empty, but a tad heavy once it was full. He took it into the living room, plugged it in, then returned to the kitchen to turn the tap on so the water got warm. He filled a bucket and staggered back to her, struggling from the weight of it, almost slopping some on her chunky bare calf. A worm-like vein stuck out of it, blue and wavy. Maybe that had happened because of her being static behind the cheese counter.

"Watch it, dickwad, you're going to spill that!"

She clipped him round the ear, and he teetered, his heart beating fast at his thought of losing even just a drop. Thankfully, he managed to stay upright and poured the water into the spa.

"What about the Radox bath salts?" she said, staring at the clear water.

He'd forgotten to add those.

"Sorry."

A quick dart into the kitchen for the Radox she kept under the sink, and the mistake had been fixed. He swished the water so the granules dissolved, then switched the spa on. She sank her feet into the blue, bubbling depths and sighed.

"You have some uses." She leaned her head back and closed her eyes. "Piss off now and make the dumplings. If you spill the flour again . . ."

He didn't need to be told what that would mean.

Careful in the kitchen, he made the dumplings and managed to keep the worktop relatively clean. He popped them in the casserole dish which had been on low in the oven all day, then whacked the heat up higher. He'd made the stew this morning before school. No praise for being able to follow the recipe in her big old dog-eared cookbook. Nothing except to tell him to add more salt and pepper, because 'No one likes an unseasoned stew, you stupid bloody moron.'

They'd be done by the time she'd finished with the spa. Another thirty minutes. He set the kitchen timer so he wasn't late going in there to dry her feet.

He tidied up the kitchen for a while then laid the table, quietly, so as not to disturb her. If he did, he'd have no dinner again, spending the evening either in the garden or the shed.

Auntie Angelica had brought something home with her today, a clear plastic box like a fish tank, a blue lid on top with a light underneath. Inside were bits of bark like you had in garden borders plus a rock, a little earthenware cat bowl beside it. What was the tank for? It sat on the sideboard by the table, taking pride of place where her large yellow flower vase used to stand.

She'd tell him eventually. He'd learnt not to ask questions. If he did, he risked a slap at worst or name-calling at the very least. Ones like devil spawn and gimp, spastic or retard. Those words were mean, cruel, and he didn't like them. He'd asked Mrs Kavanaugh about them, and she'd said if someone was calling him that, she'd need to know so she could put a stop to it, so he'd told her he'd heard it in the playground but couldn't remember who'd said it.

That made him a liar, and that was bad, too.

Seemed Angelica was right — he was bad all round. To the bone.

The egg timer went off, startling him, and he grabbed a towel then ran into the living room, drying her feet. He unplugged the spa and made a move to lift it, but she stopped him with a slap to the top of his head.

"Get on your knees," she demanded.

He did so immediately.

She grabbed his hair at the back and shoved his face down, into the blue water. He didn't struggle — that would get him into trouble, and he was hungry and wanted his dinner. He held his breath and stared at the bottom of the spa. Some bits floated, maybe flakes of her foot skin, he didn't know, but he kept his mouth shut so it didn't go in there. His lungs burned, and no matter how hard he tried not to move or fight for air, his body took over. He flailed his arms, tried to grab at her hand holding him steady, but she slapped his wrist, and it stung, stung so much.

His mouth automatically opened, and water gushed in, seeping down into his stomach, tasting of perfume. He choked, his chest constricting, and a lightness entered his head, something pleasant he was drawn to. Letting himself drift towards it, he gave up on trying to free himself. This was much nicer, the cocoon he floated into, and all the bad things that had happened to him faded away.

As he fell asleep, he smiled.

* * *

He woke with Auntie Angelica's face looming directly above his, her ruddy cheeks hanging, eyes gleaming with something he didn't understand.

"Where did you go?" she asked in a creepy voice.

He didn't get what she meant. "I didn't go anywhere. You put my face in the spa, and I fell asleep."

"And where did you go when you did that?"

He couldn't compute. Everything felt so strange, his whole body weak. "Nowhere."

"You must have."

He shook his head.

She pursed her lips. Sighed. "Then we need to try again."

She dragged him over to the spa. Dipped his face in it.

When he woke next, she asked, "And this time? Did you see a white light? Did you see your mother? Was my dog there?"

He nodded, even though he hadn't seen any of them.

"Thank God." Auntie Angelica got up and hefted him to his feet by the back of his soggy jumper. "Go and dish the dinner up now. For once, you've made me happy."

With a foggy head, confusion running rampant as to what had happened — he wasn't quite sure anymore — he did as she'd asked, water dripping from his fringe and into his eyes. A kernel of happiness sprouted in his tummy, spreading throughout him. She'd said he'd made her happy, and wasn't that just the best thing ever?

Perhaps one day he could make her happy again.

But what was the white light she'd mentioned? And why would he have seen his mum and Angelica's dog?

It didn't make sense. His life didn't make sense.

Maybe, when he was older, it would.

CHAPTER THIRTEEN

Bethany and Mike had spoken to Sunbeam again but got nothing more out of her than Bethany had on the phone. It was frustrating but couldn't be helped. You couldn't get blood out of a stone.

Now they stood at the front door of the house next to Polly's — the resident had told Nicola about a man getting out of a car and going down Polly's side alley yesterday.

At last. Something to get their teeth into.

Mrs Olive Quinto, around the same age as Polly but with a clear aversion to giving in gracefully to the grey hair, her head a cloud of bottle black, took them into a sunny kitchen. The back door was open to let in fresh air, and the yellow accents everywhere gave the room a cheery feel, which brightened Bethany's mood somewhat.

They sat around her circular pine dinner table with cups of tea.

"Mrs Quinto—"

"Olive, please." She showed off her dentures.

Bethany smiled. "What time did you see the man and the car?"

"It was yesterday, in the afternoon, but I'm afraid I don't know the time. I'd had a nap in my chair by the window, and

I'd woken up. Well, I looked out, and there he was, parking his grey car outside."

Grey. Like a million others. Fabbo.

"Do you know the make?"

"No. It was just a grey car. I didn't even notice whether it was four doors or two. I'm a little disorientated after I've had a nap, see."

"Was it on your side of the road or opposite?"

"Oh, right outside, dear. My side. I thought he was going to see Polly, but then he went down her alley instead. Behind us is a field where you can walk dogs, so I assumed he'd maybe had a small puppy with him, one I couldn't see — my hedge blocks the view of the pavement."

"Did you see him come back?"

"No. I was making some cheese and biscuits — I love Jacobs Cream Crackers, don't you? Nice bit of Lurpak on them, maybe some of that Philadelphia, the one with the chives in it. But no, I didn't see him again. He isn't from around here — I know all the neighbours by sight, and most of their visitors, too. I made it my business to study them all when I moved in. You can't be too careful, and it's best to know who you live by. When I went back in the living room after eating in here — oh, and I had a nice cup of tea as well; I used that Jersey milk, the sort where there's loads of cream in it. Don't you reckon it tastes better?" She nodded at Bethany's cup.

"It's lovely. The man . . . ?"

"Oh yes, the car had gone. I was also naughty and ate a few Ritz as well. I shouldn't, because of the salt, but I can't help myself."

"How long do you think you were in the kitchen for?"

"No idea . . ."

"What was the man like?" Bethany sipped some tea. She'd be getting some of that Jersey milk herself.

"He was tall, not an ounce of fat on him, with a big old brown beard and bushy eyebrows. Glasses, too. Rather a big nose — it looked plastic. He had a cap on, one of those baseball things. Black, it was."

"What about his clothing?"

"I'm afraid I don't remember that. I was too fixated on his beard. It was ever so long. Seems so many men have them these days, doesn't it?"

Bethany couldn't argue with that. Every other bloke appeared to have a bush on his face. "Do you recall what time you fell asleep?" That might give them an idea of what time she woke.

"I don't. My days are governed by whether my stomach rumbles, whether I need a drink, and if I'm tired, I just close my eyes. Nothing is done to a schedule now. It's marvellous. Half the time, I couldn't tell you what day it is."

"But you're sure it was yesterday you saw the man?"

"Yes, because yesterday was when the police packed up in the morning and left Ellie's house. It's so sad what happened to her."

"It is. Do you know Polly well?"

"Not really. I haven't been living here long. I had to move out of my council house because they wanted it for a family. I'd lived there all my married life and had to leave the memories behind. Still, it's nice in this street, and the rent isn't steep."

"Who do you rent from?"

"Oh, that nice Thomas couple. I can't recall the name of their business."

"Wesley and Yazeem Thomas?"

"That's them. Sweet pair. Everyone in this street rents from them. They snapped the lot up one by one, the clever buggers."

Interesting. Ellie and Polly had rented from the same place. A connection? *Did* Yazeem have something to do with this after all, even though Olive had seen a man?

They chatted to her for a little while longer, general things. Bethany wanted to waste a bit of time so she didn't appear to be breathing down Presley's neck by returning to Polly's too soon, begging for clues. With no other memories surfacing for Olive, they left without telling her what had happened to her neighbour. Olive hadn't asked either.

In Polly's house, suited and booted, gloves on, they stood in the living room with Isabelle and Presley, the dead old woman in front of them.

"She seems to have been suffocated," Presley said, moving to stand beside the chair. He pointed to the cheeks and, in the absence of the creepy white makeup, spots of red dotted her face. "Her eyes are bloodshot, and the blue around her mouth is probably a bruise from whatever was placed over her face — also the pressure from whoever held it down."

"Timescale?"

"She died yesterday, in the afternoon sometime, so if she had a hand clamped over her mouth, finger marks would be present by now. There aren't any, so I'm guessing something else was used. If a pillow, she'll possibly have minute fibres on her face. Anyway, we can better determine suffocation by testing the blood — high levels of carbon dioxide will be present."

"We'll take all these cushions in," Isabelle said, glancing at the sofa. "One may have Polly's saliva on it."

"So they changed their MO," Bethany said, "yet left clues to let us know it's them."

"Possibly toying with us." Isabelle sighed. "It's all a game to some of them. While you were gone, we had a look at what was in her mouth." She reached into her holdall and took out a clear evidence bag containing the card. "A postcard from someone who didn't sign their name, just a 'Wish you were here!', the general holiday guff. What I found interesting was the picture on the front."

She held the bag out. The postcard had been flattened, and Isabelle turned it over.

A butterfly — a Red Admiral this time, though, but maybe this was the best the killer could get. It might not be blue, but the creature was the same. Like with the daisy — a gerbera was part of the daisy family, so it was close enough to pass. Close enough to get the message across as to who had done this.

"Interestingly," Presley said, "there doesn't appear to be anything beneath her nails, so no gripping her attacker, drawing a skin sample. This usually occurs when someone is smothered while they sleep. It takes a while for the person to wake up and realise what's happening — if they even wake up at all — so she may have roused, thrashed a little, but nothing major that meant she felt she had to fight off whoever was doing this to her. She could have been in a deep sleep, and by the time she realised it was too late."

Bethany imagined the woman having a nap, probably at the same time as Olive, except Olive had been lucky to wake up and Polly hadn't.

"I just need to send Fran a message."

Bethany: POLLY DILWAY HAS BEEN MURDERED BY OUR KILLER. I NEED YOU TO CHECK WHETHER SHE HAS A LINK TO ELLIE OTHER THAN BEING HER NEIGHBOUR. ALSO CHECK WHAT COLOUR VEHICLES THE FRIENDSHIP GROUP HAVE.

Fran: OKIE DOKIE.

Bethany: AND HAPPY BIRTHDAY! WE HAVE SOMETHING FOR YOU IF WE EVER GET BACK TO THE STATION.

If we ever manage to get to the bloody shops.

Fran: OOH, THANKS!

Bethany: HOW OLD ARE YOU NOW? FIFTY?

Fran: YOU CHEEKY SOD! THIRTY, THANK YOU VERY MUCH.

Bethany sent a few laughing emojis then returned her attention to the others. "Sorry about that. What were you saying while I was using my phone?"

"Just that if Polly was asleep, maybe it saved the killer having to go through all the rigmarole of drowning her," Mike said. "If they're using a Transit, I'd say they killed Ellie and Simon elsewhere, a place where they're comfortable and have all their things to hand — the thing they drowned them in, the bugs, the gerberas, the clothing. Here, in this situation, nothing is at hand, so drowning her, although the killer's preference, wasn't something they wanted to do, especially when anyone could come along and knock on the door, and for all the killer knew, Polly could have had meals on wheels where the delivery person is allowed to use a key and come in without knocking. There's the element of getting caught in the act."

"Not to mention the amount of time it would take to drown her, bring her back to life, repeat the process, then dry her, style her hair," Isabelle said. "I'd say this wasn't on his official agenda." She lifted a hand to indicate Polly.

"I agree." Bethany nodded. "This was done to stop her saying anything about the Transit, I'm sure of it. They're afraid she would have identified them, even though it was three in the morning and dark when they dropped Ellie off."

Mike stared at the ceiling, then lowered his head. "Whatever the reason, it's done, and we need to catch the fucker before they do something else."

True. But with so little to go on, it might take weeks.

Her phone tinkled.

Fran: POLLY HAS A DAUGHTER IN NEWCASTLE. WANT ME TO GET HOLD OF THE POLICE THERE AND ASK THEM TO BREAK THE NEWS?

Bethany: PLEASE.

Fran: THE GROUP ALL HAVE SILVER CARS.

Bethany: WHAT? THAT'S A BIT WEIRD, ALL HAVING THE SAME COLOUR. WHAT ABOUT A TRANSIT?

Fran: NOPE.

Bethany: OKAY, CHEERS.

"We should be off," she said to Mike.

"Don't you want to do a house walk-through?" Isabelle frowned.

"Just a quick one. If she was killed in this chair, it's likely they didn't go anywhere else in the house."

"I know, but still . . ."

They trailed around the property behind her, Bethany's mind on visiting the remaining members of the friendship group again to talk to them about their cars and whereabouts yesterday. She'd have to warn them to be vigilant, as they might be next on the killer's list. Surely, if Olive knew all the neighbours by sight, she'd know their cars as well, therefore, she'd recognise if the grey car had been Sunbeam's and would have said so.

That's Sunbeam out of the frame then.

"That's odd," Isabelle said in the main bedroom.

"What is?" Bethany snapped her thoughts back to the now.

"There's a foot spa on the bed with blue water in it."

Bethany shrugged. "Maybe she'd used it and didn't have the energy to put it away — that's why she had a nap in her chair."

"But to leave it on a bed . . ." Isabelle shook her head. "Nope, too odd for me. You generally wouldn't put it on a bed with water in it, would you, in case it spilt onto the covers. Whatever, we'll nab it and take it in for testing, and I'll ask Presley to do a foot swab to see if her skin has any of this blue water soaked in it."

Five minutes later, the walk-through complete, Bethany and Mike took off the outer clothing in the hallway and left it in a box by the door. They went to Sunbeam's house to ask about her car, but no one was in.

Tory waved at them from across the road, then ran over. "She's gone to work then out for lunch, apparently."

"Okay. Did she say where, by any chance?"

"No."

"Did she drive off?"

"Yes, silver Kia."

"Thanks. We're off now, so as usual, if you get anything else . . ."

"I could just leave Nicola to do the rest of the house-to-house so I can stand by the victim's front door. I haven't done a log or anything. No one's signed in or out. It needs doing."

"Okay. Set one up, and we'll sign our approximate times of entry and exit."

Tory did that, and with everything squared away, Bethany and Mike got in the car.

"Let's go and get Fran's flowers now before I forget, then we can go and find the remaining people of the group and ask them where they were yesterday, late afternoon. Sod's law they all have the same colour vehicles."

"Maybe it's a coincidence."

"There seem to be a lot of those flying about in our cases. Dogs me off."

She drove to Tesco and nipped inside, selecting one of their posher bunches of flowers and a card with YOU ARE FIFTY! on it as a joke. She giggled to herself, and it was true what people had told her: *You will find things funny again, I promise.* It felt good that she had, and she smiled briefly, for once not experiencing guilt for living when Vinny wasn't.

Back in the car, she wrote in the card — *You'll be getting a Zimmer next, haha!* — then made her way to the Thomas' office first, only to be told by Wesley that Yazeem had gone out in the car.

"Silver, isn't it?" Bethany asked.

"Yes . . ."

"Where did she go?"

"Home, to change into something more comfortable. She's meeting her friends for lunch then taking the afternoon off. She's taken Ellie's death hard."

"Did you not hear about Simon?"

"What about him?"

Bethany sighed quietly. "He was also found dead in his garden. Yesterday."

"Bloody hell!"

After talking for a few minutes and getting nothing other than where the lunch was being held — at The Ringer Hotel, one o'clock — they went back to the station. A red-headed woman and a tall man stood chatting to Rob. The woman turned, and their eyes met. Bethany knew who she was instantly. What the fuck was *she* doing here? If Kribbs had gone behind her bloody back . . .

"Bethany Smith?" Ginger asked.

Bethany plastered on a smile, the scent of the flowers a bit heady. "Yes?"

"Tracy Collier." She gave a strange, tight smile, as though she didn't like showing happiness.

"Oh, hello. Come to take over my case, have you?" She laughed, if a bit unsteadily.

"Like I said to you before on the phone, not if I can fucking help it. Now, I hate it here, so if you don't mind, I'd like to get this over and done with so I can go back to my own case."

"Get what over and done with?" Bethany tilted her head.

"Giving you my advice, me saying you're fine to deal with it by yourself — two murders, isn't it? — then buggering off."

"Three murders now."

"Oh, well, however many, you can manage, can't you." Not a question. Tracy Collier didn't want to be here.

Bethany didn't want her here.

Tracy jerked a thumb at the man with her. "This is Damon Hanks, by the way. DS."

"Hi." Bethany smiled.

Mike shook his hand.

"Shall we go up to my office then?" Bethany asked. "Although I need to give these to one of my team — Fran, it's her birthday today. And I can't chat for long, as we need to get out by about one to talk to some suspects."

"Some?" Tracy looked at Damon. "See? All under control. She has *some* suspects, which is a damn sight more than we have on our case at the moment. What the fuck I'm doing here I don't bloody know."

Blimey, this woman called it as she saw it, as usual.

They trooped upstairs, and after Fran's exuberant display of emotion over the flowers and uproarious laughter about the card, Bethany led Mike, Tracy, and Damon into her office. Mike brought coffee along, and they sat around Bethany's desk on spare chairs.

"Give me what you've got. Like before, verbally," Tracy said.

Bethany recounted everything.

"I can't fucking believe I'm sitting here." Tracy shook her head. "What a waste of my time. You've got it all in hand. I've got nothing to offer you, sorry."

"Then why did you get brought in to assess?" Bethany had a good idea but wanted Tracy to tell her.

"In light of what you've recently been through, Kribbs said he was worried it would overwhelm you, plus I head serious crimes in the area and am supposed to contact you when you have them on your patch. Let's make an agreement. If you need me, give me a ring. If you're fine — then don't call." Tracy dished out another of her weird, tight smiles. "I can already tell you're like me. Trauma, go to work. Upset, go to work. Need to punch someone, go to work and hope it isn't a colleague you thump. I'm sorry for your loss, by the way."

Bethany waved it off.

Tracy stood. "Lovely to have met you, but we'll be off now."

She stood, as did Damon, who grinned as though he found Tracy utterly amazing.

And maybe she was. Just a bit alarming and hard to read.

"Oh, um, okay . . ." Bethany stood to show them out.

"Don't worry about doing that." Tracy flapped her hand. "Park your arse and have a breather. We'll find our own way out."

They left, and Bethany stared at Mike once the door had shut.

"Did that really just happen?" she whispered.

"Seems it did. Frightening bugger, isn't she." He exaggerated a shudder.

"Isn't she just, although she must have a softer side. Somewhere."

"And they left the sodding coffees."

They laughed.

"We'll grab a sandwich — I should have got one for us in Tesco — then we'll gatecrash that little lunch date." She paused, thinking. "I wonder why they're all meeting up?"

"Maybe the killer wants to figure out who to bump off next."

"Don't," she said. "I thought exactly the same thing."

CHAPTER FOURTEEN

Last night, James had spent a pleasant few hours at The Ringer Hotel, having a tasty dinner in the posh dining room then making use of the bar, knocking back a few bevvies while giggling to himself about how, there he was, a killer amongst the innocent, and no one had a bloody clue. They'd drunk their cocktails or whatever, oblivious, and laughed with their companions or talked in earnest circles. Ignorance was bliss, so they said.

He'd found himself wondering what secrets *they* were hiding. Everyone had them. Did the man in the blue suit beat his wife? Did the woman in the black dress become a social media troll when the lights went down? And the man with the strawberry-shaped nose — had to be a drinker who slapped his kids about.

Now, James sat in the dining room again, only it wasn't as relaxing as the previous evening. His nerves were strung tight, his skin crawling at being in the group's presence. He'd felt this way ever since *that* night. They'd shown their true colours.

Gavin, Sunbeam, and Yazeem sat with him at a large circular table, their faces showing their grief — pinched features, clamped mouths, sad eyes. Each had a glass of white wine, ready to toast Ellie, who didn't deserve their devotion, the bitch.

Lunch was brought out — they all had different meals, Sunbeam going for a salad with weird seeds in it — and after they'd eaten in a strange, goosebump-inducing silence, Yazeem's phone bleated out its irritating goatish message alert, which she loved and found utterly amusing. As usual, regardless of what they were doing or why they were there, she checked what it said.

Rude.

She gasped, looking up from her screen then at everyone in turn, her stupid brown eyes massive in her skinny, pointy face. "That was Wes." A pause for a hand pressed dramatically to her chest, worthy of an Oscar. "Simon's dead! Murdered!"

Dun-dun-duuuuun.

Do. Not. Laugh.

He'd keep the information to himself that he already knew about Simon, had been there in the flesh when the police had told Natasha. It was about bloody time the news had come out to the rest of them. James had been bursting to tell them since he'd offed him, and now he could watch them all crumble.

And hate them for not crumbling over the secret he'd told them.

Sunbeam did her usual dumb act and blinked into space, her brain shorting out — nothing new there. It took her a while to mentally digest emotional things, although she'd been the first to laugh at his secret. That might have been from nerves, and he'd considered letting her off, not killing her — *if* she hadn't said what she'd said later on.

Gavin reared his head back — he looked like a fucking emu with his eyes wide, his mouth a beak, sticking out where he'd pursed his lips. His sparse hair was the same as an emu an' all, more bum fluff than anything, his scalp showing through in patches, but then he had just finished chemo and it was finally growing back.

"How does Wes know before us?" James asked. "He doesn't have much to do with Simon, does he?"

Yazeem shook her head. "He said that a policeman and woman went to the office again, asking where I was."

Do they think it's Yazeem?

Super amount of LMAOs.

"Why would they want to know where *you* are?" James intended to sow the seed of doubt in Sunbeam's and Gavin's minds. Let *them* think it was her, too. It'd take any future focus off him.

He hid a wince at his thought: *Sow the seed.* Auntie Angelica had made him do that in big plant pots, and all those red gerberas had sprouted, giving off their sickly smell, reminding him he stood in a pretty garden that was nothing like Heaven but a version of Hell.

"I don't know." Yazeem tapped off a quick reply. "But that Smith woman mentioned the colour of my car to him. Why would she do that? What has my car got to do with anything?"

Fucking great. Someone must have seen him park up outside Polly's house — thank God for the beard and plastic nose. He'd have no way of finding out who it was and getting rid of them. Panic had a mind to crowd him, to grip his chest, squeeze his lungs, so it felt like he was drowning again in the foot spa, Angelica's hand on the back of his head, holding him down. Oh God, he needed to see Pretty Princess, to hear her music and see her dance so he could calm down. He hummed *Bring on the Clowns* as a substitute, his shoulders instantly lowering. He hadn't realised they'd been bunched up.

"James! How can you fucking *sing* at a time like this?" Yazeem screeched, drawing the attention of other diners.

Lots of narrowed eyes and scrunched foreheads. A tut or two. A "Really!"

"Was I? Sorry. I wasn't aware I was doing it." A crap excuse, but it would have to do. She'd never understand the power of Pretty Princess. "Nerves."

"Nerves?" Gavin took a large swig of wine.

Yes, you're getting on them.

"Nerves," James repeated. "This is a tense situation, isn't it?"

"I suppose." Gavin farted about with his fork.

"Well . . ." James went for theatrical. "If Ellie is dead, then Simon, which one of us is next?"

"Oh, piss off, J," Sunbeam said, sounding weary of him. "That's not funny."

"No, it's not," Yazeem trilled in her irate voice where it went up a few octaves and was incredibly bugging.

"It's something we have to think about," James said. He was enjoying this quite a bloody bit. "You won't be able to deny it if another one of us gets murdered." He said it like Taggart would, Scottish accent an' all. Too much? Too jokey? Yes, going by all their faces. "Sorry." *I'm not.* "I can't cope with death and tend to laugh when it happens."

Isn't that the truth.

"Yes, we all deal with it differently," Yazeem said, "but at least try to have a smidgen of respect. These are our *friends.*"

Were. Haha.

"Again, apologies. So, it seems we're raising a glass twice," James said, catching more filthy looks. "To Ellie and Simon." *Stinky Simon. Loser Simon. May you rot in Hell, the pair of you.*

The others raised their glasses, half-arsed, genuinely morose. Shame they couldn't have pasted on the same expressions when he'd revealed his nasty childhood. None of this would even be happening if they'd given him a shoulder to cry on, showed a *smidgen of respect.* It was all their fault. This. All of it.

"Oh, this is horrible, what's happened," Sunbeam wailed.

Not half as horrible as you lot.

"Yes, dreadful," James said. "I have to say I'm worried."

"What about?" Gavin brushed a hand over his patchy hair.

"Being killed." *Muhahaa.*

"Pack it in," Yazeem said, her hand shaking, wine sloshing in her glass. "You've got *me* panicking now."

So you should be. I'm coming for you next. See you later, tater.

"Well, I'm going to carry on as normal," Gavin said. "I've looked the prospect of death in the face once already, so I'll do it again."

You keep dreaming, mate.

"Coffee?" James asked.

Everyone agreed, and once the waitress had brought them over, cups brimming, along with a full carafe for top-ups, that weird silence came back again. James got the sense these people didn't like him anymore, just tolerated him, the same as Auntie Angelica had. What was wrong with him to make people feel that way?

Mrs Kavanaugh didn't. She was nice.

The first cups had been swallowed, and Gavin poured seconds.

The double doors to the dining room swung open, and in walked those detectives, Smith and Wilkins. Shit. James kept his expression neutral as the pair headed their way. Had Wes blabbed about where they'd be? Of course he had, the law-abiding twat. What did they want? If they were disturbing their lunch, it had to be serious, didn't it?

Was this the end? Would he be caught before he'd had a chance to get rid of everyone?

Fuck it.

Smith stood beside Gavin and observed them all for an unnerving moment, then, "Sorry to interrupt, but it's easier if we see you all at the same time. Mr Obbington already knows, but for the rest of you: Are you aware Simon was murdered?" She explained when that had been.

Yazeem gave James a scathing look.

Now you know how it feels to have news kept from you.

Wilkins sat on the spare seat and took his notebook out. Smith stared at them all in turn. Everyone admitted they knew — via Wesley.

"Where were you on the night in question?" Smith asked. "You don't have to answer that, Mr Obbington."

Great. The rest of the group would want to know why. He'd have to tell them he'd already been asked when at Natasha's. Then they'd be curious as to why he'd been there. Bloody hell!

Another mean look from Yazeem.

Oh, fuck off, you're boring me.

"I was at home," Sunbeam said. "Carly was round. She stayed the night; didn't want to leave me on my own after finding out about Ellie. You can ring her if you like."

"We will." Smith smiled at her as though Sunbeam wasn't a suspect. "What about you, Gavin?"

"At my nan's. She's in a care home. You have to sign in and out, and there's CCTV." He smiled a smug smile — you can't pin this on me!

"We'll look into that, thank you. And you, Yazeem?"

"At home with Wes and our next-door neighbours. They came round for drinks."

"Names and address, please."

Wilkins appeared an eager beaver, his pen poised over his pad, ready to scribble the information down. Yazeem told them what they wanted to know, and to anyone listening, everyone was covered. None of them could have killed Simon.

I'm safe.

"Where were you late yesterday afternoon, Mr Obbington, after we'd seen you?"

His guts dropped. The question threw him off, and he almost allowed his emotions to slip onto his face. "Let me think . . . Hang on, I'll check my phone diary." He took it out and accessed the app. "Ah, assessing a house for renovation. It's on the outskirts. Jamberwell Road, d'you know it?" *Where there are no CCTV cameras for you to know whether I was there or not. No other houses along that stretch. Fuck you.*

Smith nodded. "And the rest of you?" She raised her eyebrows.

"At my shop," said Sunbeam.

"At a property with clients, showing them around," said Yazeem.

"And the clients' names?" Smith cocked her head then smiled when Yazeem provided them. She looked at Gavin.

"Nan's again." He smiled.

"You go there often then?" she asked.

"Every day."

"That's lovely of you. Now, your cars . . . Were any of you in Ellie's street yesterday, apart from Sunbeam?"

Ah, they'd probably discovered that Polly woman. Each of them shook their heads except for Sunbeam.

"I was," she said, "but I found her, so . . ."

James' heart pitter-pattered painfully — he hadn't expected the nosy old bag to be discovered so soon and wondered why Sunbeam hadn't mentioned it before now.

"Okay, thank you for your time." Smith gave a curt nod. "Please be aware that whoever is doing this may come for you next. Stay safe. Make sure you're always with someone."

She strode away, and Wilkins got up, following along behind her, sliding his notebook into his pocket. Despite Smith's parting words, it was clear to James that the gang was under suspicion — but which one did they think had done it? With no proof, they couldn't pin it on anyone, so he reckoned he was in the clear. He'd sneak out through the back of the hotel later, walk over the scrubland by the river, and get in his car in the residential street beyond.

Plan still on track.

"Well," he said. "That was a bit weird, asking us about being in Ellie's street."

"It wasn't," Sunbeam said. "Polly was killed yesterday."

"Who's Polly?" Gavin asked. "I forgot."

"A neighbour." Sunbeam's ponytail shivered. "She's the one who saw the Transit parked outside Ellie's. I spoke to one of the uniform coppers, and she said Polly had been murdered."

"Oh, that's dreadful," Yazeem said, hand on her chest again.

"Are they supposed to tell you that sort of thing?" James asked.

"Probably not," Gavin said, "but maybe she said it to see Sun's reaction."

"Reaction?" Sunbeam's eyebrows wiggled. "What for?"

"To see if you killed her." James almost choked on suppressed laughter.

"Me? What the hell would I want to do that for?" Sunbeam's eyes darted about. "I wouldn't hurt anyone."

But you did. You hurt me. So much.

"So if the neighbour saw the Transit . . ." Gavin leaned back, head in the emu position again. "Then she was bumped off because Ellie's killer thought they'd get caught if she lived and told the police what she knew."

"Quite the detective, eh?" James chuckled, glad none of them had thought to question him as to why he hadn't had to explain his whereabouts.

"This isn't funny," Yazeem snapped. "What the hell is wrong with you lately, J?"

"I've told you. Nerves." He wanted to slap her. He wanted Pretty Princess.

"Look, why don't we all take a moment to calm down." Sunbeam's ponytail swung as she glanced round at them all.

It was becoming annoying. He'd enjoy grabbing it when he shoved her face in the foot spa.

"Good idea," he said. "This is all getting a bit scary." *For you lot.*

A few moments passed with them all drinking their now tepid coffee, thanks to Smith's interruption. James entertained tonight and how Yazeem would respond to his request that she say sorry. Even if she did, he was going to kill her anyway. He just wanted to hear the words, from one of them, didn't matter who.

"I'm going home," Yazeem announced. "I'm taking the afternoon off, and I have yoga later."

I know.

"Enjoy that," he said.

Everyone got up, and after a round of goodbyes and fake hugs, Sunbeam, Yazeem, and Gavin left. James asked for the bill, paid, then walked out to reception.

"Could I order room service for dinner later?" He gave a big smile to the woman behind the desk.

"Oh, Mr Obbington. Do you feel better now?" she asked.

Good. She'd remembered him from when he'd told her he wasn't to be disturbed by housekeeping.

"Much, thank you, although it tired me out, being poorly."

"What would you like?"

"Something light. A tuna salad, perhaps." No heavy homemade chicken pie to weigh him down while he drowned Yazeem. It had been a mistake to eat it before getting rid of Simon.

"Anything for dessert?"

"No, thank you."

"And what time would you like your meal?"

"About seven. Is it okay for me to leave my plate outside the room rather than have someone knock for it afterwards? I need an early night and don't wish to be bothered."

"Of course! That's booked for you." She gave him a massive smile.

"Great, I appreciate it."

He left to go to work, satisfied everything would go to plan. It was convenient he could slip out via the back door later and not be seen. Like he was meant to do this. No obstacles. No finger of blame pointing at him. No remorse.

He'd become Auntie Angelica.

And he shuddered at the thought.

CHAPTER FIFTEEN

In the downward dog position, Yazeem tried to let all the stress float out of her. It wasn't working.

"That's it," the instructor, Zoe, crooned. "Let it gooooo. Imagine it rising, rising, rising, out of you and into the ether."

She reminded Yazeem of an Earth lover, the sort who banged on about vibes and energies emanating out of people and into you. And, alarmingly, Zoe put truth into the theory that empaths existed and felt what you felt. She always knew when anyone in the class was upset, zeroing in on them and talking until they confessed. In that case, she'd head over to Yazeem in a minute and get everything off Yazeem's chest before she even knew it had happened.

Shit. She didn't want to talk about it tonight, not after finding out about Simon. Okay, he'd been a knob for the whole time she'd known him, right from a kid, but he was still her friend. And she was worried that what James and Smith had said could be true: one of them might be next.

She wouldn't entertain that. She wanted to have kids with Wes now their business was off the ground and thriving. They had so much to do. If she got killed, Wes would be distraught.

"And breeeaaatheeeee," Zoe said in her hypnotising voice.

A sharp noise came out of someone's bottom. That was the trouble with yoga. No one giggled, just kept breathing.

"Now, on your backs." Zoe glided around, wafting her hands in a ghost-like manner. "And just close your eyes and sink into yourself. Into the real you. Let everything go, from your head to your toes. Relaaaaaaaaaax your shoulders, feel the tennnnnsion dripping out of you and into your mat."

Normally, this worked for Yazeem, but tonight, her muscles refused to obey the instructor. She opened her eyes, stared at the ceiling, and concentrated on the rectangular tiles.

"A problem, Yazeem?" Zoe sat cross-legged beside her. "Your aura is buzzing, and it's gone dark, so dark."

Dear God.

"Let's talk it out." Zoe clasped her hands behind her neck, baring extraordinary lengths of armpit hair.

She could plait that.

"Close your eyes again and tell me what's wrong. It will free your chakra, cleanse your mind and leave you fresh and relieved."

Like she wanted to fall into that trap. When this happened to others, everyone in the room heard what was said. It was the highlight of the night, soaking up someone's previously hidden secrets, and she always tuned it out because it reminded her of when James had spilled his. Of course, he was making it up. There was no way he'd have stuck it out there once he got old enough to leave. They'd all laughed, telling him the joke was over, he could stop mucking about now, but he'd got well angry, and that had them giggling even more.

What if he'd been telling the truth, though? He hadn't been the same since.

Yazeem wasn't prepared to bare all to Zoe. She didn't want her grief and fear known by anyone else apart from Wes and the gang. It was too personal. Too raw. She was in mourning, not on Zoe's version of Jeremy Kyle's old stage.

She closed her eyes. "I'm fine, thank you."

"No, you're not."

Zoe's exhale fluttered over Yazeem's bare stomach, and she wished she hadn't worn a short sports top. She willed herself to relax, but having Zoe so close meant she couldn't. Unable to bear the silent, unseen scrutiny, she calmly got up, gathered her shoes and bag from by the door, and left.

Zoe's distraught "Yazeem?" followed her.

She felt bad, but sometimes, things got too overwhelming. She'd recognised the fight, flight, or freeze options barrelling towards her on that mat, and flight had won.

Out in the balmy evening air, she took a deep breath and slid her trainers on. She didn't want to go home yet, and there was still half an hour of the class left. Wes was normally the one person she dashed to if she felt this way, but for some reason, she didn't want to burden him with it and preferred to be by herself.

There was a late-night bistro up the road, where one section was for coffee drinkers and readers, or people needing a moment to sit with a cuppa and whack out their laptops. She made her way there, paid for a latte, and sat in the far corner, away from everyone else.

To think. To breeeeeaathe. To relaaaaaaaaaax.

* * *

Gavin had had a tough old time of it lately and needed someone to talk to. With no wife or kids, he was a bit of a lonely bastard, and Mum and Dad had buggered off to live in New Zealand a few years back, so their place wasn't an option either. He'd seen them just after chemo had stopped, though, so that had been nice. A flying visit, but better than none at all.

Out of all the members of their group, he liked Yazeem the most, always had. She seemed to understand him more than the others and had sat with him on a few chemo sessions, reading from the latest book they'd chosen. Sunbeam had popped to his house once with one of her weird salads, so he didn't have to cook when he was so tired, and Ellie had been a rock, sending him messages of support and offering to move in with him for the length of the treatment so he wasn't going through it alone. He'd refused, not wanting to be a burden, but it had been a wonderful gesture.

He missed her.

James and Simon hadn't seemed to give a toss about Gavin's diagnosis, and it was weird that out of a group of people, he'd bonded with the women the most. Mind you, once it had become clear Simon was into booze and drugs, Gavin had tried to steer clear, and James was so intent on making money he didn't really have time for any of them these days. Nice that he'd bought them lunch, though.

Gavin got up off the sofa and decided to go and meet Yazeem. She'd mentioned yoga earlier, so maybe she'd like a quick drink in the bistro after. He needed to get things off his chest, his feelings about how he was devastated at losing Ellie but didn't care one way or the other about Simon — and it bothered him. They were mates, had been for years, and he should feel *something*, surely, but Simon had changed so much he'd become unrecognisable, someone Gavin wouldn't choose to be friends with.

He got on the bus, taking the short trip to the community centre — walking took it out of him at the moment, and he didn't fancy driving after he'd had wine earlier. He didn't trust himself behind the wheel anyway, what with sometimes feeling so weak. Once he arrived, he waited outside, glancing at his watch. Ten minutes, and she'd be finished. She'd help him get through this like she had with the chemo, although he had yet to find out whether he'd beaten the disease. He had a scan next week that would reveal whether the tumour had shrunk or gone completely. Yazeem had said she'd go to the appointment with him and hold his hand in case it was bad news.

He leaned on the wall and stared across the road at the park they used to play in as kids. They'd meet up, drinking Coke and sharing sweets, crisps, then later, as teens, trying out smoking and cider for the hell of it. Sunbeam hadn't liked either, preferring to treat her body as 'a temple' as she'd put it. She'd probably got that bollocks from one of those magazines she loved so much. It surprised him that she desecrated her temple with nights out on the lash, *and* she'd had wine at lunch. Nowt queer as folk.

The memories tumbled in, and he smiled at the night Ellie had spun herself on the roundabout so many times she'd puked up all the White Lightning. She said it would put her off overdoing the booze for life. Simon had laughed and called her a lightweight, and Yazeem had dubbed him a pig for being so mean.

It had been that day they'd all agreed to buy silver cars when they grew up, cementing their friendship further, showing the world they were united, even with their vehicles.

Gavin smiled. They had been such good years, then they'd got older, branching off into their own lives, only getting together once a month for a meal at each other's houses or The Ringer Hotel, a promise they'd made one day in the summer holidays: Never lose touch. Stay friends forever.

If only they'd known back then what would happen. It was hard to believe Ellie and Simon were gone. What if James and that policewoman were right? What if someone intended to pick them all off one by one? That would mean they had a mutual enemy, and he couldn't think who it might be. Certainly not one of the gang. They were too close for that.

He stared down at his feet in deep thought, losing himself to images flickering inside his head of them all laughing, messing about or listening to music in Yazeem's childhood bedroom, the only parents who'd let them gather in their home as a group.

Those were the days.

"What are you doing here?"

Gavin snapped his head up. James stood there, frowning, hands in the pockets of his black jeans. He didn't look too happy, but then he never did lately. He'd had a rod up his arse ever since he'd told them that bullshit story about his aunt treating him badly. Gavin didn't believe it. The woman had been nothing but kind to them and had even given them money for lollies from the ice cream van once. She'd been nice taking James in after his mum had died. No way she could be mean if she'd done something like that. And anyway, once James had said he'd wet himself in the garden, that had been it. Everyone, drunk as skunks, had roared. Maybe they shouldn't have, but it had been *that* funny.

"Oh, um, waiting for Yaz," Gavin said. "Why, what brings you here? Unusual for you to be back on the old stomping ground."

James lived in the better part of the city, what with all that money he had. Yazeem had stayed here, same as Gavin, even though Yaz could afford a big house of her own now.

"I wanted a trip down memory lane." James smiled, if a tad tightly. "Then I remembered Yaz was at yoga and thought we could have a chat about a business venture I have in mind."

James' eyelid twitched. It always did when he was lying. It had flickered at lunch as well, several times, albeit faintly.

"What sort of business venture?" Gavin asked.

"Me buying a few houses like she did in one street, doing them up really nice, then getting her to deal with renting them out for me." He scowled as though he thought Gavin had no right to know.

"Great idea."

A stream of women came out of the door beside him then, and he pushed off the wall, waiting to spot Yaz. She wasn't there, so he asked a black-haired lady, "Was Yazeem Thomas here tonight?"

She nodded. "Yes, but she left early."

Bloody hell. "Okay, thanks." He turned to James. "Wonder where she went then. I'll give her a ring."

"Nah." James clapped him on the shoulder. "What about us getting together instead? We could go to mine, sink a few beers."

Gavin thought about James' swanky house and how at home he always felt there. "All right then." He smiled. "Beats being alone in my place."

* * *

James handed Gavin a sixth beer laced with vodka, naffed off he'd had to switch kill nights over. He'd looked forward to grabbing Yazeem's hair all day, and now there was Gavin, with nothing that James could hold on to except a few poxy tufts. Still, he'd get the pleasure of hurting Yazeem tomorrow evening instead. She had swimming then. He'd just have to hope Wes didn't go with her like he sometimes did. That could really balls things up.

Angry about it, he plastered on a smile to hide the rage, listening to Gavin warble on about how he was afraid to die if the cancer didn't go away. James wanted to tell him to be grateful the big C wouldn't be the thing to finish him off, and that his imminent death would be much less painful, but of course, he kept that to himself.

With Gavin deep in his cups, James said, "Do you remember that night when I told you my secret?"

Gavin grinned. "God, that was hilarious, wasn't it? And you thought we'd *believe* it. I liked your auntie. She was well nice."

She wasn't. She was hideous and wicked and so very cruel.

"I've got something to show you in the garage." James couldn't wait any longer. It had been three hours of reminiscing, and that was about all he could handle.

"What's that then?" Gavin got up, stumbling a bit.

"You'll see."

James led the way, clenching then unclenching his hands, fury simmering just below the surface, ready to burst out as soon as he called on it. He walked around the van quickly, waiting on the other side for Gavin to appear. James slipped on his latex gloves. They'd give him a good purchase on Gavin's scalp.

Gavin lumbered into sight and stopped short, staring at the floor. "What's with the plastic sheet?"

"Forget about that. Come over here a second." James moved to the table with the foot spa on it. "What do you think of this?" He leaned over the spa, but to one side.

Gavin weaved up to it. Bent over, too. "It's blue water." Then he looked at James, and the realisation of its significance widened his eyes.

Ellie and Simon hadn't made the connection.

"That's like the spa in your story," Gavin said. "That had blue water as well." His slurred words sounded like he'd had just enough booze to prompt him to apologise.

"It's exactly the same spa." James inhaled. Exhaled. "The blue is—"

"Radox. That's what you said, didn't you?"

So he'd been listening back then. Had taken it all in.

"Are you sorry for laughing at me?" James asked, switching the spa on.

Gavin said much the same as Simon had, about it not being their fault James had had a shitty upbringing, then added, "*If* you even had one. Sorry, mate, I just can't see it. I mean, who makes a kid stand in the garden for hours or shoves them in a shed with spiders and shit? And who puts people's faces in foot spas?"

A heartbeat. Then, "Me."

He grabbed Gavin's head, slamming it down, water sloshing out of the spa. Getting behind him meant he'd have more leverage, plus Gavin's useless flailing wouldn't touch him — the bloke had weird short arms. He seemed unable to reach backwards enough to grab at James, who stood a step away.

"Say sorry," James whispered in his ear. "All I want is for one of you little fuckers to . . . Just. Say. Sorry."

He waited for Gavin to go limp, then hauled him down to the floor. One of Gavin's elbows whacked against the Welsh dresser, and a paint can toppled off, reminding James of when Simon had been here. CPR was creepy with Gavin's eyes wide open like that, but James got on with it, squeezing Gavin's nose harder than he should but needing to take his anger out on him. After two lots of chest compressions and breathing air into his mouth, nothing had happened, so James worked on.

This time, there was no repeat face dunking. No apology again. There was nothing left but to wash him, put on the suit, shirt, and shoes, the makeup and the lashes, the insects in his ears, then take him home to the garden at his place.

To not see Gavin come back to life upset James more then he thought it would. The evening hadn't gone as planned at all, thanks to Yazeem.

How disappointing.

He'd enjoyed cutting out Gavin's tongue, though.

CHAPTER SIXTEEN

Bethany stood in the incident room, studying the whiteboards. They were crammed with information and a photo of each of the deceased. A new day might see results, but she doubted it. After their visit to the friendship group at The Ringer Hotel yesterday, they'd returned to the station, Mike helping Fran and Leona with the various checks, Bethany going to her office and sorting out her paperwork. She hadn't filled out her daily reports like she usually did when on a case and had needed Mike's extensive jottings from his notebook to recall what time they'd visited people for questioning and what had been said. Chief Kribbs would ask her if she was coping if he knew she hadn't been on the ball, maybe suggest she take the rest of her bereavement leave. Fuck off.

That job had taken her until the end of the shift. Fran had searched CCTV outside Mezzo's where Ellie was supposed to go with her date. She'd arrived then walked down an alley. With the others in the team no farther forward, they'd called it a day.

She'd gone home to her empty house and cried upon catching the scent of Vinny's coat hanging on the hook by the door. She supposed she'd have to sort his clothes and belongings out, but not yet. No, not yet. Too difficult.

Painful. And it would be admitting the truth fully. That he was gone. Never coming back. If his things were around, she could pretend. Tell herself he'd gone away on a long course for the fire service. Anything. Something.

So far, this morning had been based in the station, mired in clues but no leads. Ellie's parents had been informed of her death and were coming to the UK from Cyprus, boarding a flight tomorrow, the earliest they could get. Polly's daughter was arriving from Newcastle later in the day and said she'd go straight to her mother's house if the police had finished there and start packing it up, worrying she sounded heartless but needing to do it quickly because of work and child commitments. Bethany had assured her not to feel bad, that it had to be done at some point because the house was rented, and now was as good a time as any.

Shame she couldn't take her own advice.

She sighed. "Vin, this is utterly shit without you," she whispered, so low she hoped no one else heard.

No answer, not even his voice in her head.

She dipped hers and closed her eyes, not wanting the team to see the tears. They'd worry, fuss, and she didn't want that.

Switch your mind to work.

She scanned all the data in front of her. Fran's and Leona's persistent digging had found nothing with regards to motive — it seemed no one would have wanted to hurt Ellie or Polly, although Simon was another matter altogether. People from his Facebook friends had been spoken to over the phone, and a few of them weren't surprised he'd been killed, saying he was always annoying someone, mainly asking for money, tobacco, booze, and weed. He'd dabbled with it all as a teen but had gone further, making it a daily habit instead of recreational.

One man had said he was tired of Simon treating Natasha the way he did. Had someone killed him because of her? But what about Ellie? No, Bethany didn't think it was anything to do with Natasha.

She saw now, reading one of the boards, that Fran had already looked at that angle. She'd phoned Natasha and asked her outright. Natasha had got along with Ellie and had no reason to kill her.

The gerberas, insects, and method of murder hadn't drawn any solid conclusions either. She'd bet they'd be something relevant only to the killer. The clown makeup and mouthpiece — what did they mean?

The words becoming a jumble, Bethany left the incident room and went into her office. She did a search for Zebedee Hollingworth, and while she didn't want to question him again, she *did* want to find the man he sold drugs for. A quick scroll through his arrests showed that last year, Zebedee had been brought in on suspicion of selling weed He'd been picked up on a street corner, appearing to hand out small baggies to people as they supposedly shook hands, under police surveillance. A man had been with him, one 'Uncle Crack', aka Rick Attenborough, the pun of his nickname probably intended regarding drugs, but neither of them had anything on them, and the photos that had been taken couldn't prove drugs had exchanged hands.

She exited her office and walked over to Mike's desk. "I'm probably clutching at straws, but we have an uncle to visit."

He frowned up at her, then scribbled a few notes on an A4 pad. "But none of them have uncles, we checked."

"I know. It's another kind of uncle. It's what he calls himself. Uncle Crack, for God's sake."

"Why do we need to see him?" He closed his email browser. "Leona, can you carry on with this CCTV, please? I'm trying to find silver or grey cars. I've put it on the pad here how far along I've got and what streets and dates have been ticked off."

She got up and smiled, stretching. "Yep, a change would be good. I'm only doing the far past for each victim and coming up with nothing."

"I'll take over that," Fran said. "I'm done with social media. If I see one more emoji, I'm likely to scream."

Bethany fluffed up her hair. It had been sticking to her neck, the fans in this place not doing much to cool the rooms. "We're off to see Rick Attenborough, the man who's suspected of supplying the drugs to Simon's dealer. He may have had reason to kill Simon, and for all we know, the others in the group might also use drugs. Unlikely, but I'll take any theory and run with it at the moment. He's on the Shadwell Heights estate."

"Ooh, dodgy area," Fran said, sitting at Leona's desk while Leona went to Mike's.

"Yep, but if I can just get him off our list, we can concentrate elsewhere."

"I'm telling you, I have a strong feeling it's one of the friendship group," Leona said.

Bethany nodded. "I feel the same, but they all have alibis. I investigated them thoroughly. And shit, I need to add that info to the board." She went over there and scribbled it all down. "Okay, Yazeem's neighbours who came for drinks, one of them is a magistrate, so I think we can take his word for it that they were there. CCTV shows Sunbeam at work — lucky for us the camera on the other side of the road points directly at her florist shop. Gavin was at his nan's care home; the manager distinctly remembers him because he always takes the staff sweets to share, and on the days in question he'd brought a box each of Quality Street and Jelly Babies — it stood out to her because he usually buys bags. Sounds like a pretty nice bloke. Olive Quinto said a man had gone down Polly's alley, but that he had a plastic-looking nose. It could be a woman in disguise; fake beard. What's next? Ah, here we are. The Ringer Hotel confirmed James was in residence and is down as being there for the foreseeable. The leak at his house must have been bad."

"Hmm, well, someone is lying." Leona rolled her shoulders. "You wait and see."

"I think you're right," Bethany said. "It's just a case of catching them out on something. If we get nothing from whatever today throws at us, we'll go and see them all again tomorrow on the pretext that we want them to think properly about whether anyone would want to do this to their friends."

Fran and Leona bent their heads to their tasks — end of the discussion then.

Bethany and Mike left the station, arriving on the Heights estate within ten minutes, a grotty place that had once been shiny and new in the fifties but had seriously gone downhill. The council were slow to act on repairs, and the streets had more potholes than smooth tarmac. All right, a bit of an exaggeration, but that was how it seemed. The houses themselves had ancient windows that needed replacing with double glazing, and some front gardens resembled the rubbish tip.

Uncle Crack lived in one of the high-rises — grey, pebble-dash affairs that appeared to lean over if you looked at them from a certain angle, like five towers of Pisa. Balconies lined the buildings, concrete walkways to the front doors. He was on the fifth floor, so they rode the piss-stinking lift, even though Bethany hated them. She didn't have the energy to tromp up all those stairs.

On his level, people were out in force, probably Uncle Crack's lookouts. A skinny blonde woman leaned on her doorframe, smoking a cigarette, hair in the staple messy bun. A child played in the folds of her long denim skirt, maybe a year old, naked except for a sagging nappy hanging off her arse, her hair in pineapple-sprout pigtails. Several youths kicked a ball up and down the top end of the walkway, and two men rested their forearms on the balcony rail, nonchalant, making out they weren't up to no good.

"Are you ready for this?" Mike asked while they paused outside the lift.

"Reminds me of being back on the beat, coming here. Yeah, let's get it over with. I'm going with the same attitude as I had with Zebedee, just so you don't think I've gone mad. I want information at this time and have no interest in pulling Uncle Crack in for anything — unless there's drugs out in the open that we can nab him on. We can't ignore that.

But in their absence — what we don't see won't hurt us, if you catch my drift."

"What," he said on a laugh, "you think he'll let us in?"

"He'll probably try not to, but I'll give it a go — might have to threaten for entry."

"I thought you said you'd be treating him like Zebedee?"

"I did, but I realised I might have to let him think otherwise. I'll play it by ear."

They walked past the woman, who blew fag smoke in their faces. People around here scented 'the filth' a mile off, so Bethany wasn't surprised at the gesture. It was designed to tell them exactly what she thought of them, and Bethany didn't care one iota. She was on the right side of the law, and the woman probably wasn't.

The men previously lounging stood straighter, in an I'm-well-hard stance, watching from the corners of their eyes, trying to seem as though they weren't. They happened to be right outside Uncle Crack's door.

A bit unfortunate.

Bethany knocked on it.

"He's busy," one of the men said, then sucked his teeth.

"I'm sure he is, but so are we." She stood side-on and smiled at him.

"No one round here got time for no pigs," the other said, looking her up and down, trying to be intimidating but coming off as a prat.

She'd let it go, what he'd said — unless either of them pushed it.

A boy opened the door, about seven or eight, blond, podgy. His shorts and T-shirt, grubby as eff, had her wanting to buy him new clothes. Maybe he'd been playing out today and had got dirty.

He grinned, a front tooth missing, the one next to it in need of a dentist the rot was that bad. "What d'you bleedin' want, and what's your name?"

"I need to speak to Uncle Crack."

"Wait there." The kid pushed the door to.

Bethany sensed the stares of those on the balcony, and the lads had stopped playing football, the walkway now ominously pin-drop silent. She kept her attention on the door, while Mike leaned his back on the wall beside it to keep an eye out. It would be stupid if both faced away from the residents interested in their arrival.

The boy reappeared. "What's the word, dog?"

Dog. Lovely. And she needed a fucking password. "The words are Detective who isn't here to cause trouble."

Someone shifted — probably the man who didn't have time for pigs. She glanced at Mike, who stared ahead, face hard and unreadable. The child went inside again, then came back, opening the door wide.

"He said to go in."

"Thank you."

They stepped inside, and the kid pointed to a door at the end of the hallway. A kitchen, seeing as a sink unit was in view. Mike went first, giving her the signal that it might not be safe, and she followed him into the room. It wasn't obvious Crack earned a fortune from drugs, but it was no shithole either. He was keeping it 'normal'.

Uncle Crack sat at a black dining table, a calculator in front of him as well as a ledger, a smoking cigarette hanging from his mouth. He was the opposite to the boy — slim, clean, and had all his teeth from what she could gather by the shape of his jaw. His black hair was in a fade, Tommy from *Peaky Blinders*, and he looked a bit like him when she squinted. If he had drugs in here, they weren't evident.

The quicker she could get answers, the quicker they could leave. She was uneasy now they were in his home.

She showed him her ID. "We're not here for you, okay?"

He stubbed his fag out in an ashtray, smoke curling in a blue-grey stream. "Then what *do* you want?"

"Information on Simon Knight."

He chuffed out a breath that might have been the start of a laugh. "What about him? Dead, so the rumours say."

From Zebedee, no doubt.

She nodded. "Do you know of anyone who might want to kill him?"

He smiled, enigmatic, alluring. "Me now, but he can't be killed twice. I prefer people who acquaint themselves with me to be alive. Want a list of potentials?"

"If you don't mind." She squirmed beneath his visual scrutiny. He had the knack of creating an atmosphere, one she wasn't comfortable with.

"I'm joking. I don't have a list. It's probably someone he bought goods or borrowed money from."

"Goods?" She held her breath for his answer. Would he admit it was drugs?

"You know exactly what I'm talking about."

That's a no then.

She had to push for more. "Okay, do you have a name you can give me?"

"Nope. I can't do that." He spun the calculator around.

"What *can* you do?"

He lit another cigarette. She was strangely drawn to him in a fascinated-by-a-suave-drug-dealer way. He had charisma, and it disturbed her that he had enough to lure people in, getting them hooked on drugs. She could well imagine women falling for him.

He studied her through a haze of smoke. "I could tell you that he lives on the Ring Road estate, but I won't. I could tell you he drives a black BMW with personal plates spelling out his moniker, but I won't. And I *could* tell you Simon owed him about a grand the last I heard and was paying it off in instalments of about fifty quid a fortnight, which is why the skanky fucker never had any money, and also why he started coming to me, but I won't tell you that either."

"Thank you." She turned to leave.

His eyebrows crept up, and a sardonic smile tweaked his lips. "What, that's it? You don't want to give me a lecture, warn me off my profession?"

"No. I came for information only. I got it. Now we're going."

"Fuck me, a copper who tells the truth." He stared at her with his mesmerising blue eyes. Chilling. "Do me a favour, will you?"

God, he was a bold bastard. So laid-back and sure of himself.

"What's that?"

"I'm going to have to tell people you came here to search the place — I've got a rep to uphold. I don't fancy people accusing me of being a snitch. I'd appreciate you going along with that — and also not going to see him until later so I've got a chance to get the word out. As in, ring him and tell him you were here. I'll have to say you're doing the rounds of all the people like me."

She nodded. "Fine."

"I might have to shout something as you're leaving an' all," he said. "For authenticity."

He gazed right into her soul, and she found it difficult to look away.

Mike cleared his throat, breaking the trance.

She left the room before Crack could reel her in with his eyes any longer. The boy opened the front door, chewing on a Snickers, and they stepped out onto the balcony. Relief filled her, and she shook off the spell Crack had put her under. What the hell was wrong with her?

Uncle Crack shouted, "If you keep coming round here bothering me, I'll have you for harassment, you fucking pair of cu—"

The door snapped shut. The men leaning on the balcony laughed. Bethany and Mike walked away, the fag-puffing woman no longer there, but her child sat on the doorstep eating a bag of white chocolate buttons. The football was kicked, and it smacked into the back of Bethany's leg. She kept going, refusing to turn and give them an excuse to hassle her.

Mike prodded the lift button, and they stepped on after a tense minute or so of listening to pig snorts and ribald hoots. She only relaxed when they were back in the car, which had a few kids surrounding it, all of them staring through the windscreen, menacing, lawless, and completely without fear.

"Let's get the fuck out of here," she said, shivering, and drove towards the Ring Road estate, dreading what they'd find there, what kind of reception they'd get. She knew exactly who Crack had referred to. Fuck waiting until later to see him. Crack would have rung him immediately, and she didn't care what she'd promised.

Turned out the man in question was on his drive polishing that BMW of his. "I heard you were coming, and it wasn't me, so fuck off."

Bethany believed him. Like Crack, he had a nonchalant air about him, and it was clear he didn't give a shit about their presence, wasn't jittery or acting as though he had something to hide.

"Do you know of anyone who would have killed Simon?" she asked.

"No," he said, the circular movements of his hand inside a polishing glove bringing a beautiful shine to the bonnet. "But whoever it was has cost me money. He still owes me six hundred quid. So I'll be putting feelers out as to who did it an' all, because now *they* owe me that money."

Bethany and Mike left him to it, no farther forward, Bethany still jittery from her encounter with Crack and the people on the walkway. Thank God she didn't pound this beat anymore. She pitied the coppers who did.

CHAPTER SEVENTEEN

James stood in the shed. Auntie Angelica hadn't left yet, though, and it was dark with the door shut and the torch off, so he couldn't see a thing. Pretty Princess danced in the swarming blackness, and the music played, soothing his ragged nerves somewhat, although not completely. Auntie Angelica hummed along with the tune. She'd brought the tank in with them, and it had been covered with a cloth for about a week now.

"If you lift that cloth and peek underneath, I think I might finally kill you." That was what she'd said when she'd first covered it.

He hadn't touched the cloth. He'd stayed away from the tank as much as possible.

"Guess what I have in my tank," she said now.

He had to do what she said, otherwise there would be consequences. "Um . . . uh . . . a snake?"

"No. Try again."

He needed to pee. "A lizard?"

"Oh no. Something much smaller. And it can do all sorts to you if it bites, although you won't die, and that's a pity, isn't it. If you don't upset it, you'll be fine."

"I w-won't upset it." His knees knocked together.

"If it nips you, you'll go numb there. You might even go dizzy and be sick. But you mustn't be sick. You know how much I hate that."

"O-okay . . ."

"Get on the floor. Lie down."

He did, shaking, so frightened. Clenched his fists by his sides. Held his breath. Scrunched his eyes closed. Waiting, waiting, waiting for her to put whatever it was on him. Then it came, two hard and heavy thuds on his chest, and he thought she might have tipped the whole tank contents on him. The hard things must be the earthenware bowl and the rock. His eyes snapped open, even though he didn't want them to. Something scurried up his neck, onto his cheek, its legs tickling his skin — an insect? Oh God, what had she put on him now? — and it came to a stop over one eye.

"Say hello to False Widow. And be good. I'll be back later."

The creak of her winding up the jewellery box was loud and threatening this time, not the usual calming sound he looked forward to and needed. He imagined Pretty Princess spinning, her tiny lips pulled up into a serene smile, but it didn't dispel the terror careening through him, sending him hot and shaky.

Auntie Angelica switched the torch on. James stared at what looked like a giant eyelash that had come loose to rest over his eye — thick, furry, some kind of insect leg. And what he thought might be a bulbous abdomen. He'd seen the likes of it before, just not so big. He remained still, not wanting the creature to bite him.

The door shut behind her, and he was left alone, wishing he was in the darkness again so he didn't have to see the partial of what sat on his face. He didn't dare close his eyes. It might upset the thing.

It moved, crawling down his cheek, scuttling to his chest, then hurrying across to flicker over his arm and away, thank God, away, towards Pretty Princess. James shot to his feet, the bowl, rock, and bark pieces scattering, and stalked the little beast, a big spider, which crouched next to the jewellery box. He couldn't let it bite Pretty Princess. So he raised his leg, bent at the knee, stamping down on the fat bastard and swivelling his foot, just to be sure. The spider popped, and James watched it replay in his head, as though he'd actually seen it from someone else's point of view, his sole coming down, crushing the widow. He scraped his shoe on the floor, a shout of revulsion coming out of him, then grabbed the jewellery box and retreated to a corner, keeping an eye out for more spiders.

He sat for a long time, watching, searching.

Nothing.

He kept seeing the leg, the eyelash, like it was still there, and the footsteps of the spider, he still felt them, featherlight touches, gentle yet so frightening.

Time passed, he had no idea how many minutes or hours, but he'd wound the jewellery box up too many times to remember and had fallen asleep somewhere along the line. Pretty Princess had danced and danced, the melody calming him. Then the shed door swung open, and she *stood there, a clear-blue sky behind her head, and clouds, lovely, fluffy clouds. A summertime sight.*

So he'd been there all night.

The scent of gerberas came in, and his stomach rolled over. Nauseated, he swallowed down bile.

"Did it bite you?" she asked.

"No," he said.

"Fuck." She sniffed, hands on hips. "Come on. It's time for school."

CHAPTER EIGHTEEN

In the car, Bethany's phone rang. She managed to get it out of her pocket while driving and handed it to Mike. "Get that for me, will you?"

"Says Front Desk on the screen."

"Fuck."

He swiped it and put the mobile to his ear. Bethany remained facing forward, taking a moment to steel herself for what Mike would tell her once the call was over, but she had a feeling she already knew.

"Mike here. Beth's driving." He drummed his fingertips on the side window. "Seriously?" He let out a huge sigh. "Where?" A long pause. "Bloody hell's bells! Okay, we'll go there now. Cheers." He popped her phone in the drink holder between the seats.

"Do I want to know?" she asked.

"No."

"But you'll have to tell me so I can drive there. Which one is it?" She knew it had something to do with the friendship group. Another body. Another frustrating day ahead of them, not knowing what the hell was going on, who was doing it, and why.

"SOCO are already there, as are uniforms, and Presley's on the way. The address is Gavin's."

"Wonderful." She did a U-turn at the end of the road and went back the other way. "Leona was right; I was right. Something is definitely going on with that group. There are three left — James, Sunbeam, and Yazeem. One of them might be a killer, and if it wasn't a woman in disguise at Polly's, it's James."

"Or it could be someone from school, holding a grudge because they wouldn't let them into their gang. You know how weird kids can be. Or it could be . . . oh, I don't sodding know."

"Wesley? No, scrap that. Their magistrate friend gave him an alibi. I'm talking shit, ignore me. Your school kid theory could hold water, but why wait all these years to do something about it? Again, ignore me. Some people hold on to slights forever before they act."

"Maybe something triggered them, set them off. Trauma — a death, divorce, whatever. Weird things can happen when you're upset. Stuff festers silently then bursts with an outlet."

Was he giving her a personal warning veiled as them talking about the case? Did he think she'd do 'weird things' because of what had happened to Vinny? "If you wanted that to be double-edged, you succeeded, but I don't feel the remotest need to do weird things."

"What? I didn't mean you. Christ! If I did, I'd have said so."

"Sorry." Guilt piled into her. "I suppose I'm still sensitive."

"Well, don't be with me. I'm a straight shooter, you know that. Anything I have to say, I'll say it to you and make sure you know it's directed at you."

"Okay, let's start again. Rewind the conversation." She bit her lip to stop herself from crying those stupid tears that seemed to want to surprise her so much lately with their uninvited appearance. "We'll say it's one of the remaining friends who's done it, regardless of gender. Yazeem has a strong alibi — unless the magistrate is lying. Sunbeam, too — unless her friend, Cathy, is lying. So that leaves James, and the hotel staff said he was there."

"He could have sneaked out. The receptionist might have nipped off for a wee or something, left the desk unmanned."

"Hmm. Sounds plausible. We should go there and check the exits, see if he could have left without notice. After we've seen if this is Gavin who's dead, obviously. He *is* dead, isn't he? That's what the call was about?"

"Yep."

"We're almost there." She took a right into his street, Hillsop Rise, and headed for twenty-two. Last time they'd been here she hadn't suspected him at all, and she'd been right not to — unless he'd topped himself, unable to bear the guilt of killing his friends, knowing it would only be a matter of time before he was caught.

She parked behind the SOCO van, and they got out. Bethany sent a message to Fran, telling her Gavin had been killed and to get on with finding his parents so they could be informed.

Nicola Eccles came over from across the road, and Bethany met her at the kerb.

"A neighbour saw a Transit parked out here last night," Nicola said. "About two in the morning."

"Okay, give Mike the address for that person, will you? And the name. Thanks."

Bethany walked up the path towards Tory, who always seemed to wangle herself a spot at the front door as the guard and person in charge of the entry and exit log.

"Hi, Tory. I see there's no alleyway, unlike the others, so I assume we'll be going through the house, unless there's another way round into the rear garden. Assuming he's in the garden, that is."

Tory nodded and pointed to a box of protective clothing, then got the log out ready. "Yes, he's in the garden."

"First on scene, were you?" Bethany took out two outfits, booties, and gloves.

"Me and Nicola, yes. The next-door neighbour reported it, number twenty-one. She has a key in case Gavin needed her."

What would he need anyone for?

Mike moved to stand beside Bethany, and they togged up.

"Did she say why he might need her exactly?" Bethany asked.

"No, and I didn't push for an answer because she was too upset. Thought you'd like to deal with her."

"I will."

They signed themselves in, and Bethany led the way.

"Straight ahead is the living room, and there's a set of patio doors," Tory said.

"Thanks."

They walked along the hallway, Bethany glancing into a kitchen on the right — messy, food cartons and cans left out on the worktops, dirty saucepans on the hob, the sink full of filthy crockery, and two SOCO mooching about. She entered the living room, which was just as grotty, and marvelled at how people could live in a hoarder's paradise without feeling as though it cluttered their mind as well as their home. He hadn't cleaned up since they'd visited him the other day. It wasn't as gross as Simon's, though.

The patio doors stood open, letting in the fresh air, turning the room from the musty stench it had been before into something more breathable that didn't have her hiding a retch. She stepped outside onto a slim path that spanned the width of the house, grass stretching back beyond that, right to the bottom where the photographer snapped away beside Isabelle inside a tent, the flaps open, a sour expression contorting her face. A shed stood to the right, and an empty plant pot full of weeds sat in front of it, a plastic gerbera pushed into the soil. The sight of it got right on Bethany's nellies because she still didn't know its significance.

Isabelle turned and waved them over. Bethany walked between SOCO on their hands and knees searching the grass and came to a stop inside the tent next to Isabelle, Mike arriving a second later. The interior was cool, thank goodness.

The photographer clicked once more, then, "That's me done out here." He strode off towards the house.

"Well, this is nice seeing you so often, but what with the last serial killer and now this, your mug is becoming a bit too familiar." Isabelle chuckled. "Only joking."

"I was going to say, the same could work the other way round." Bethany smiled. "What do you reckon then?" She pointed to the body without looking at it, unsure if she could stand seeing another clown face and whatever insects had been put on and in him.

"Same as the others. Nice suit, like Simon's — dark blue, but the red tie is in his pocket, the end hanging out. The makeup is the usual, right down to the blue eyeshadow and the line moustache, and there's the flower, although that's in a pot this time. His gob is wide open with one of those bloody mouthpieces again, and the blue butterfly is easily seen — as in, it's not down by his throat. He has earplugs, but we'll wait for Presley to see what delights are inside. Oh, and Gavin has the top four buttons of his shirt undone, his chest on display, unlike Simon's, which was buttoned to the collar. A rush job? Did they get disturbed and have to stop dressing him before someone caught them?"

Bethany took a deep breath and stared at Gavin's face. His patchy hair was a sight, and she wondered whether he suffered from alopecia. Yes, the white makeup and blusher circles on the cheeks were there, as was the drawn-on moustache, and one of the butterfly's wings peeked out, resting on his bottom lip. His eyes were wide open, and they had the look about them of a startled, frightened person. Had he been so scared while being drowned that it had resulted in this expression — if, indeed, he had been drowned?

"I don't know," Bethany said. "It's a good theory, which suggests, if he was disturbed, that the kill was done where others are around, or at their house and someone came to the door."

"It's like he's purposely in a state of undress," Mike said. "Listen, if you think about it, everything about this killer tells me what they've done is for a reason. I don't buy your theory, sorry," he said, shrugging at Isabelle. "Gavin's clothes are meant to be like this."

Bethany was inclined to agree but didn't say so. Isabelle was uncharacteristically blushing over Mike rejecting her musings. Did she have a thing for him? Bethany smiled at the thought.

Presley's voice floated from inside the house, and Bethany faced the patio doors, peering through the tent opening, dreading it if he was in a pissy mood again. She could normally handle him, welcomed his attitude, but at the moment, she was fragile and took his jibes to heart. She inhaled a deep breath and held it until he joined them.

"This is becoming tiresome," he said and placed his bag on an evidence step beside Gavin.

"What, seeing our faces or the actual death?" It had come out of her mouth before Bethany had a chance to rein it in, and it told her Isabelle's words earlier had struck a nerve. *What's the matter with me?*

"Both." Presley hunkered down next to Gavin. "And that was a joke. I really mean just the death. I'm dogged off because I have these three friends on my workload, Polly Dilway, plus the usual. Others do die, you know, and they need my attention, too."

Bethany bristled at that. "It's not like we ask for murders, is it? Hey, Killer, do your worst to upset Presley Zouch, because it's fun winding him up. And that *wasn't* a joke." She folded her arms.

"I'm sorry," he said. "I've forgotten to make allowances. Forgot you might not find me amusing at the moment."

Remorse flooded her. She'd come back to work, said to Kribbs she was fit for it, and here she was, telling people not to treat her differently but expecting it anyway. "I apologise, too. If I can't handle the usual, I shouldn't be here." The urge to up and run overcame her. It was strong and seeming to shove her in the back, but if she did that, what did she face? An empty house smelling of Vinny, memories, and the constant reminder that he wasn't there. No, she needed her work. *Had* to be here or she'd go mad.

Mike squeezed her hand.

"Let's move on. I'll do an ear temp once I've checked them for bugs." Presley did his usual with a catcher box beside Gavin's head, removed the plug, and peered inside. He inserted tweezers and brought out some insect or other. "A cricket. Lush." He popped it in the box and did the same on the other side, this time removing a few dead earwigs.

"Ugh, for God's sake," Bethany said.

With the tubs sealed, Presley took the temperature then stared at the sky, clearly working out the time of death in his head. "Same as the others. Last night, evening." He picked up Gavin's hand. "Rigor is gone." Then he shone a torch at the nostrils. "Ooh, what do we have here?"

Bethany's stomach clenched, and she squinted, as if that would help her cope with what he pulled out. Presley manipulated another insect from the left nostril, a moth with its wings close to its body, and it appeared dried out, as though it had died a while ago. She imagined the killer catching all these creatures as and when they needed them. What message were they trying to get across?

"Fuck's sake." Mike coughed. "I bloody hate those things."

"Whoever is doing this isn't getting the bugs from the victims' gardens," Isabelle said. "From the thorough checks we've done of Ellie's and Simon's, nothing has been dug up, no earth disturbed to collect things like worms. No pots moved to find ants or woodlice, so I'm confident they're being sourced from elsewhere — probably their own garden."

"Changing the subject," Presley said, inspecting Gavin's scalp, "he's recently been through chemo, I'd bet my rep on it."

"So not alopecia then?" Bethany asked. How had she got it so wrong?

"No, this is patchy regrowth from treatment."

"He never said to us he had cancer." Then she berated herself. Why *would* he tell them? Now she thought about it, it was obvious why his hair was like that, and she kicked herself for not cottoning on before so she could have offered him sympathy while he'd been alive. It wasn't much good to him dead, but she gave him a silent apology anyway. "This is doing my nut in, I have to say. I just can't get everything linked together." She lowered her voice owing to possible eavesdropping neighbours. "Though I'm convinced it's one of the others, if you see what I'm saying."

"That's obvious." Presley leaned over Gavin and sniffed his chest. "Same soap used to wash him. If you'd just get up the courage to smell him, Beth, you might recognise it as something you've had a whiff of while speaking to the other friends."

She widened her eyes in alarm. "Sorry, I'll do everything I can to solve a case, but I am *not* sniffing a dead body." *You should. It's your job.*

Mike stepped forward. "I'll do it."

"Thank you." Bethany turned away while he got down on his hands and knees. She stared out into the garden.

A SOCO dusted for prints on the patio doors. Whoever this was had to have brought Gavin out through the house. So they had a key — but then they'd probably have one anyway, taking it out of Gavin's pocket at some point. But they'd have to know where all the victims lived, so it was plain as day the killer knew them all or had been following them. If it wasn't one of the friendship group, it would be someone else linked to them. Social media and old-fashioned digging hadn't thrown up anyone it could be, though, and she gritted her teeth in annoyance at that.

"Nope, I haven't smelt that before," Mike said. "It's like some sort of thing that'd be called Ocean Breeze or whatever."

She turned to face the others again. "The house," she said, looking at Isabelle. "Can we do a walk-through now? I have the next-door neighbour to speak to — the one who spotted him out here — plus someone who saw a Transit."

Isabelle nodded, and they returned inside to be given the tour, which didn't throw up anything obvious except no sign of forced entry. The upstairs was just as much of a shit tip as the rest of the place, and by the time Bethany and Mike had logged out and stood on the path in the front garden, she felt dirty and clammy.

"Right, moving on . . . Twenty-one first." She stripped off her outer clothing.

They placed their protectives in a black bag and made their way to see a woman who had seen much the same as Polly Dilway had.

Let's hope she doesn't get killed for it, too.

CHAPTER NINETEEN

Auntie Angelica had let a man into the house. He stood there in the living room doorway, his dark-blue suit immaculate, as was his crisp white shirt buttoned right to the top, a red tie resting down the middle. His Adam's apple was big, peeking over the collar, and his black shoes shone in the slant of late-evening sunshine coming through the slatted blinds. James wondered whether they were new or just polished regularly. He had black hair and a thin moustache, like it had been drawn on with a pen.

"This is Brett," Angelica said, waving her hand in a flourish as though the man was a prize. "And he'll be here all evening, which means you can't be."

She stared at James, her eyes wide, that blue makeup on the lids stretching up high. He knew what she was implying without words. He'd have to go and stand in the garden or sit in the shed.

"Is he yours?" Brett asked, clearly startled by James being there. "You said you didn't have children." He frowned at her and ran a hand through his hair.

"I don't," she said. "It's my sister's."

It?

"Oh, that's okay then." Brett pulled a weird face. "I don't do kids."

"Me neither." She glared at James. "Go on, scoot off home."

Home was the shed. She'd said so often enough. It was where he belonged, apparently. He trudged out of the house and into the back garden, his feet so heavy, the air still so warm that the scent of those horrid flowers sailed up his nose. God, he hated them.

In the shed, he settled down with Pretty Princess and listened to the music, thankful no bugs were in attendance. His stomach growled, and he guessed the meal he'd made — spaghetti Bolognese — wasn't meant for him and Auntie Angelica after all but for her and that bloke. James had browsed her cookbook to try something new, and it was easy enough to make, and they'd had all the ingredients. Now, he'd never know what it tasted like. Not until he made it again at any rate.

Mrs Kavanaugh said he was a clever boy being able to make meals like that.

He wished she was his new mum.

He told himself to expect a long evening, maybe the whole night if Brett stayed over. Anger towards Brett surged. If he hadn't turned up, James might not be out here. He'd have a full belly and could sleep in his bed, not be starving and propped up in this wooden corner with only Pretty Princess for company.

He detested his life.

Why did Mummy have to go out that night to a fancy ball for work? Why had the driver been drinking? He'd mown her down as she'd crossed the road to get to the venue, smacking into her at too many miles per hour, sending her flying through the air to land on a brick wall, her body draped over it like washing on a line. Auntie Angelica had liked telling him that bit, and the picture it conjured in his mind replayed sometimes, a flickering photograph, Mummy's long red dress ruched up to show one slender leg, her sparkly Dorothy shoe on the end of her dinky foot, the other lost somewhere when she'd been thrown aloft. Her handbag — he'd imagined it in the road, the contents scattered, a lipstick here, her compact mirror there, her small purse open, coins spilling out.

She'd looked like a queen that night, and he remembered telling her that before she'd floated out of the door, her dress swishing. His babysitter had read him stories about a hungry caterpillar, and another that was based around all the insects in the garden you could imagine. Wilf the Worm, Martha the Moth, so many of them. They were nice creatures, not like the real ones.

He rubbed his eyes, angry that tears had come. The tune from the jewellery box stopped, and he wound it up again, then bent his legs so he could perch it on his knees. Pretty Princess spun around, and he spotted himself in the little mirror behind her — mottled cheeks, red-rimmed eyes — and abhorred what he saw. A child without a mother he'd adored, a mother who wouldn't be saving him from this life. She'd never wrap him in her arms again, or sing to him, or soothe his worries.

All he had left was Angelica and her huge nostrils, her spite, and her disgust for him.

He drifted off to sleep, and however long later, was roused by the opening of the shed door.

"There you are!" Brett said, out of breath as though he'd been running, torch in hand, shining it in James' face. He turned to the right, peering around the edge of the open door. "Here he is, Gelly."

Gelly?

"Oh, you daft boy," Auntie Angelica said, nice as pie, appearing next to Brett, her hair all over the place, a dressing gown wrapped around her. "I told you to go home."

He didn't answer how he wanted — This is home, you said! — and instead stared, not wanting to say anything in case it was wrong.

"Come on, you'd best get inside." Brett held out a hand. "Won't your sister be worried, Gelly? It's past midnight."

"She'll know he's here, don't worry."

Auntie Angelica was good at lying.

James took in Brett's rumpled shirt, undone nearly to the waist, the end of the red tie dangling out of his trouser pocket, the rest of it creating a bulge. He had no jacket on, and two spots of dark pink, almost perfect circles, sat on his cheeks. His skin seemed unnaturally pale in the moonlight, giving the impression the man was a clown. James glanced at Auntie Angelica, who still sported her hideous blue eyeshadow, and tiredness hazed his vision, the two faces merging as one. Brett now had blue eyelids, thick lashes, and it was so strange, so unsettling, that James needed the loo.

He got up and followed them back to the house, hating Brett for being there, hating Auntie Angelica for inviting him, giving James another spell in that wicked shed that he disliked so much.

She ushered him to bed in the 'spare room', which was really his, but she was playing games for Brett's benefit. Beneath the covers, James listened to her saying goodbye to the man at the front door.

Why had Brett even been looking for him if he thought James had gone home? It didn't make sense. Had Angelica wanted to get rid of Brett so had made up some story that James had stayed out there, hiding in the garden? Maybe Brett had seen him walking into the garden through the kitchen window from where he'd stood in the hallway at the living room door earlier, and it wasn't until much later that he'd twigged the garden didn't have a gate for James to leave by.

James didn't know, and he tumbled into sleep, too exhausted and hungry to care any longer.

CHAPTER TWENTY

In number twenty-one Hillsop Rise, Bethany sat in Mrs Lifton's living room, the cream leather sofa nice and soft, the throw cushions like gentle arms pressing into her sides. The brown-haired woman, about fifty-five, had made them a Tassimo coffee and, despite initially being shocked about Gavin, she was thankfully okay now, if a little watery-eyed. Mike had opted for a chair opposite, and Mrs Lifton perched on another beside the fireplace.

"Thanks for this," Bethany said, raising her cup, the scent of coffee strong and enticing. It was too hot at the moment, though. She didn't fancy scalding her mouth.

"Oh, you're most welcome." Mrs Lifton nodded.

"Sorry to have to ask questions again when you've spoken to our colleague already, but if you could just go through it once more, we'd really appreciate that." Bethany smiled.

"Well, as I said while I was making us these drinks, I saw him when I opened the bathroom window. Then I moved into the spare bedroom out the back and got a better look. He was just lying there, you know, in a suit, and I wondered whether he'd been to some do or other last night, because he went out, you know, but he wasn't wearing those clothes. No, he had jeans and a T-shirt on, with trainers."

That got Bethany's attention. "What time was that?"

"Oh, after seven. He caught the bus at the end of the street."

"Why would he do that? He owns a car, doesn't he?"

Mrs Lifton nodded. "He does, it's that silver one out the front, but he gets tired easily at the moment, what with the chemo, so he worries he'll fall asleep at the wheel. Sensible chap is Gavin."

"Do you recall anyone visiting Gavin who also has a silver or grey car?"

"Oh yes. There's that nice Ellie and Yazeem. Oh, and that Sunshine woman, bubbly as anything, if a bit empty in the head. They all have silver ones, and they've been so good to Gavin, especially Yazeem."

"Anyone else? A man maybe?"

She shook her head. "No, just the girls. Well, I say girls, they're women, but you know what I mean."

Bethany smiled again. "What about a Transit? Have you seen one of those?" She purposely didn't mention the colour or the time it had been spotted.

"No, sorry." She sipped her coffee.

"Does anyone else live here who might have seen something?"

"No."

"Do you know Gavin well?"

"Yes, but only because he lives next door. I helped him out from time to time with meals and things while he was going through treatment, and I went to the shops and whatever for him when he didn't have the energy. He gave me a key in case he got lightheaded and fell over. I'd hear him, the walls are that thin in these houses, and if I didn't, he said he'd text me to ask for a rescue." She smiled sadly. "He never did fall, so there was no need for me to use the key." She sighed, her fringe lifting with the exhalation. "I can't believe he might have beat cancer only to be dead anyway."

"Do you know of anyone who would have wanted to do this to him?" Bethany took a mouthful of her drink. Bloody gorgeous.

"I don't. He has a lovely friendship group, so he told me, known them since they were kids, and that's where Ellie, Yazeem, and Sunshine come in."

Bethany waited for Mike to correct her — Sunbeam, not Sunshine! He didn't, and she hid a grin at his knowing smirk.

"Do you know anything about Gavin's family?"

"His mum and dad live in New Zealand. I know that because they came to stay recently after he'd been told about the cancer. A lovely couple. They brought me a bunch of flowers for watching out for Gavin. Really no need, but it was a sweet gesture. Just a flying visit, they said, but it perked him up no end. Such a shame he didn't get to know whether his cancer had gone before this happened. He was due for a scan soon to see if the tumours have decreased or gone. Such a worry for the poor thing. Did it get him in the end, do you think? I mean, I wondered if he'd collapsed when he got home last night, which was about two, because I heard a car engine and the front door open and close. Maybe he'd gone out the back to get some fresh air." She frowned and pulled at her bottom lip. "Hang on, the front door opened and closed twice, and the same with the back. What was he playing at?"

"We don't know, Mrs Lifton. We're in the dark as much as you are." A partial lie.

There wouldn't be much more they could get out of Mrs Lifton, so they drank the rest of their coffees while she reminisced about Gavin, dabbing at her eyes with her fingertips, laughing one minute, upset the next. They left her with condolences, which reminded Bethany of all the people who'd said 'Sorry for your loss' to her. How easily she'd fallen into the same trap here, forgetting it had upset her something chronic.

Sorry didn't make it better in her case. It didn't bring Vinny back.

Mike checked his notebook. "We're dealing with a man, eighty-seven, a Harold Thatcher, number forty-six."

"Related to Margaret?"

"What?" He frowned, looking both ways to check it was clear to cross the road.

"You know, Margaret Thatcher, the old prime minister."

"Oh, piss off, you silly sod."

She laughed, dipping her head so no watching neighbours got the idea she thought this mess was funny. Up the path in an immaculate, worthy-of-a-medal garden, she pressed the doorbell, and the *ding-dong-duh-ding-dong* floated out to them.

An elderly man answered, smiling to reveal ill-fitting dentures. His white hair was thick for a man his age, swept to one side, some sort of product on it, comb lines perfect. He reminded her of that fella who played the old wizard in the *Harry Potter* films and was dying to ask Mike who that was but couldn't. Round glasses perched on the bridge of his nose, prevented from falling down by a knot of cartilage in the middle.

Bethany showed him her ID. "Hello, sir. I'm DI Bethany Smith, and this is my colleague, DS Mike Wilkins. Mr Thatcher, is it?"

"Yes, no relation to Margaret."

Mike coughed, and Bethany cleared her throat to rid it of the giggle sitting there.

"Please may we come in?"

"Yes, of course. I've just boiled the kettle." He shuffled back to let them enter.

"Oh, not for us, thank you," she said, standing in his hallway, her belly still warm from Mrs Lifton's coffee. "We've just had one at your other neighbour's."

"Okay." He closed the door.

He appeared so crestfallen. Bethany felt sorry for him and thought maybe he didn't get many visitors. Maybe today was the highlight of his week with so much activity in the street.

"Oh, go on then," she said. "But just half a cup." She might have to ask to use his toilet at this rate.

He brightened at what she'd said and took them into the kitchen with its wallpaper that had flowers all over it and a sideboard that must have been fashionable in the nineteen-twenties. She let him waffle about things 'In my day . . .' while he made the drinks, then they went out into a beautiful back garden where he obviously spent a lot of his time. The grass wasn't fake but looked it, every strand cut to the same level, and the flowerbeds were a riot of colour, a rockery with the blooms starting low at the front and getting taller the farther back they went.

"What a lovely little haven you have here, Mr Thatcher," she said, taking a seat on one of the two white wrought-iron chairs. It was hot from the sun and burnt her bum.

"That'd be Henry to you." He winked and sat opposite her.

Mike perched on a bench under the kitchen window, notebook out, as usual. A bee decided to bumble around him, and he gently wafted the air to send it on its way.

"Okay, tell us about this van, Henry." She leaned back a bit, enjoying the break in such nice surroundings.

"It came about two in the morning. I'd got up to use the toilet — the bladder at my age is unforgiving and doesn't tend to wait like it used to, but that's by the by. I left the bathroom, and headlights shone through my bedroom curtains, so I looked out to see what was going on. Well now, someone had backed up in front of Gavin's, the lad with cancer. I thought it was a coroner's van at first, but a man in dark clothing got out, and I know that because he'd parked directly beneath a lamppost."

Her heartbeat escalated. *A man.* "What happened next?"

"He walked to the back of the van, disappeared for a moment behind the doors he'd opened, then came back into view, going up to the front door and using a key to open it. He returned to the van and carried something over his shoulder on his trip back to the house. I rather thought it was a sack of some kind, or perhaps a rolled-up carpet, a rug, and as he had a key for Gavin's, I assumed it was one of his friends. I went back to bed. Has something happened?"

"What colour was the van, Henry?"

"Ah, classic deflection. You didn't answer my query." He gave a sly smile. "I was in the army so know all about questioning tactics. So something has happened. What a shame. It was a Transit, probably white as it was bright under the streetlight, and no, I couldn't make out the reg number. It was covered up, possibly dirty."

"Thank you. Yes, unfortunately, Gavin has been murdered." She pondered on whether to tell him about the others and decided against it.

"Oh, dear God, how awful." He blinked a lot and seemed unable to form any more words, until, "So what I thought was a sack or carpet . . ."

Bethany nodded.

"Terrible business."

"I'm afraid so."

They drank their tea in silence, the sounds of summer creating a musical backdrop — that bee humming, a wasp buzzing angrily, starlings on the fence squawking, someone using a lawnmower.

"I've just remembered something," Henry said.

Ooh! "What's that then?"

"I'm so sorry, I don't know why I didn't say so before, but I was just sitting here thinking about it, watching it in my head, so to speak. After he'd taken the 'carpet' inside, he came back out to the van, then went indoors with what appeared to be a shoe box with something resting on top, although I couldn't make out what that was."

A shoe box? Polly had seen the killer carrying a box outside Ellie's as well. "Anything else?"

"No."

"Well, thank you for the tea. May I borrow your toilet?" she asked.

"You can't borrow it, but you can use it."

She smiled and went inside, Mike following. After they'd finished, she walked into the kitchen to pop her head out of the back doorway to say goodbye to Henry. Then they left the house to go to Gavin's, put protective gear on, and went into the garden again. She dipped into the tent and looked at Gavin's shoes. They weren't new, so why the box? The beige soles had black patches from where they'd got the most wear.

"Can you remember what Simon's and Ellie's shoes were like underneath?" she asked Isabelle, seeing as Presley was nowhere in sight.

"Worn. Why?"

"Shit." Bethany rubbed her forehead. "I was hoping they were new so we could search sales like we did with the last case." She clenched her teeth, waved at Isabelle, then buggered off to take the protective clothing off out the front.

Mike did the same, and they got in the car, Bethany thinking about all they'd learnt today since they'd been at the station. Hours had passed, so she drove off, heading for a small café on the estate where they could get some lunch. Once they'd ordered, carried their tray over, and had taken their seats, she gave Fran a quick ring to update her.

"Leona just got a break on CCTV," Fran said. "She's spotted a Transit driving past the shops on Gavin's estate."

"We're actually there now, in the café — we missed lunch."

"We nipped out to the bistro down the road and had cream cakes. I bought one each for you two."

"Thank you! Okay, so the CCTV?"

"Yes, the van drove past, caught by the camera outside the newsagent's. Can't see the reg number, but the vehicle was there around two-thirty this morning."

"That ties in. It was seen outside Gavin's around two, so that gives whoever was driving it enough time to despatch the goods in the garden then leave." She couldn't speak freely as the café bustled with customers. "Okay, did you rewind to see if it had gone past earlier than two, as in, while it was on the way to Gavin's?"

"Yes, and nothing. However, with the direction it was leaving, it's given us a chance to study the map. Either the person lives on Gavin's estate or the next one along, and that's where James Obbington lives."

Bethany's stomach hollowed out, her heart banging away. "Okay, that estate is the posh one, yes?"

"Yes."

"Right, we'll go out there for a drive in a second and check the houses in his street, see if there's any private CCTV. Thanks for that info, you've made my day. Can you message me his address, please? Catch you later." She got up, putting her phone in her pocket. "Lunch on the go, mate."

Mike sighed. "Thought that was what you were going to say."

She took their plated sandwiches to the counter and asked for them to be wrapped up. With that done, their coffees poured into to-go cups, they exited the café and climbed in the car. Bethany opened her sandwiches and rested them on her lap, driving away towards the next estate, taking a bite of her cheese and tomato on brown while she was at it.

"Oh, my phone," she said, a tone trilling. She took it out of her pocket and handed it to Mike. "Can you check my messages, please. Fran's sending an address."

He knew her passcode and plugged it in. "Are you going to tell me what's going on?"

"Fuck, I forgot." She explained what Fran had told her. "So we're going to James' house, something we haven't done yet because when we first met him, he was at Natasha Vanton's, if you remember."

"James? Bloody hell. I don't know why I'm surprised." He prodded her screen a few times. "Number seven Brollworth Mews." He placed her phone on his thigh.

She stared at it for a second, like he was. Ah. Her message list was up, and there were some there from Vinny that she couldn't bring herself to delete.

He cleared his throat. "Do you need to talk—"

"Don't," she said. "I'm fine, and if I'm not, you'll be the first person I run to, believe me."

He put the phone in the cup holder. "Okay."

"Brollworth Mews, eh? Might have known he'd live there. The biggest houses in the bloody city. Let's hope one of his lovely neighbours has CCTV, and if not, they might have spotted that he has a Transit — if it's him."

"I'll give him a good old sniff when we see him next and tell you."

"Eh?" She frowned, turning right.

"To see if he smells the same as Gavin."

"Oh. That." She bit off a piece of sandwich. "Shut up. I'm eating."

He laughed and munched on his own — ham and pickle with some crispy lettuce hanging out of it.

She found Brollworth and pulled up outside number twenty, at an angle and opposite James' so they could sit and finish their food while studying the street. All the homes were beautiful and had to cost close to half a million, maybe more. She stared over at James' place — large driveway, double garage, a tree standing on its own patch of grass in front of what might be the living room windows.

"CCTV over there," Mike said, pointing to number three.

"Fucking ace," she said and grabbed her coffee. "A quick swig or two, then we'll go over there and ask if we can view the video. We just have to hope they're in."

CHAPTER TWENTY-ONE

James had drunk too much. So had everyone else.

They'd got together for their usual monthly gathering, and tonight, more than any other, James wanted to blab. About everything. Several times this evening he'd almost said something, but they were all in an extremely silly mood, so maybe it wasn't the time. He needed them drunk, but serious. When people were drunk, they showed their true colours and had the urgent need to apologise for everything. He needed them to do that, to say sorry, because Auntie Angelica never had.

If only one person did, it wouldn't seem so bad.

Gavin poured another round of vodkas. "Let's tell some stories about when we were kids."

Sunbeam held her hand up. "Me first. I used to stare up at the sky at night and pretend I was an alien who couldn't get home."

Much laughter followed.

"Not like that," Gavin said. "Serious stuff. Something we haven't told each other."

"What d'you want to know that sort of thing for?" Simon asked.

"Bother you, does it?" Gavin scratched his head. "Got some deep, dark, thieving secrets, have you?"

Simon blushed. "Okay, here goes. You know that night we got lashed up on cider at the park and that woman walking through had a go at us and said we were disgusting?"

Nods. Yeahs.

"Well," Simon went on, "I followed the bitch home, and because it was summer, she went in her house and opened her living room window. I waited for her to leave the room then put my hand in and nicked her phone off the sill."

"You what?" Yazeem said, eyes wide. "That is really bad. What did you do with it?"

"Sold it to some other kids for a tenner. I got myself a KFC bucket with it." Simon laughed, showing his dreadful gums.

"What about you, J?" Gavin asked.

It was now or never, wasn't it? They wanted a secret, so they could bloody well have it. He cleared his throat. "After my mum died, as you know, I went to stay with my aunt. She abused me."

"Get out of here," Simon shouted, a bit too over the top.

"What sort of abuse?" Yazeem asked, eyeing him over the rim of her glass like she didn't believe him, her eyes twinkling.

"She used to make me stand out in the garden for hours. I wasn't allowed to move, and she locked me in the shed, overnight a lot of the time. She put spiders and insects on me, said I was a naughty noodle."

Someone made a noise as if holding back laughter, but he couldn't work out who it'd been.

"I used to piss myself because I was so scared," James said.

Sunbeam let rip, cracking up, her mouth wide, eyes shut, the bitch. What was so funny?

"You pissed yourself?" she said. "Like, proper down your legs?"

James nodded.

"Oh, you naughty noodle," Simon quipped.

He told them more, and that was it. Everyone except James roared come the end of the telling. They found his wretched childhood amusing. They were showing their real selves, what they felt, and it was just as wicked as Auntie Angelica had been.

"You're a liar," Sunbeam said. "That's a made-up story if ever I heard one."

James had never felt so alone or helpless, more so than when he'd been a kid. Here he was, a man, and he should be able to cope with it all by now after having years of practice, but it had taken a lot of guts for him to confess, and he'd thought they'd have comforted him, said they were shocked at what he'd been through: God, we're so sorry, J.

He got none of that.

Anger simmered, mixed with shame and embarrassment. It wasn't his fault he'd wet himself. He was so young, and he hadn't been able to hold it.

"That's gross," Gavin said once he'd calmed his giggles. "Do you still piss yourself now if you stand about for too long?"

James stared at him. "You lot are sick. What I've told you is serious."

"If it was that serious, you'd have gone to the police or something." Simon again.

"Forget I said anything." James hung his head and stormed out.

But he wouldn't forget.

No. Never.

CHAPTER TWENTY-TWO

In the neighbour's, looking at the monitor in a Mrs Urshwin's home office, Bethany stared in astonishment. James Obbington did indeed own a Transit, although that fact hadn't shown up when Fran had done the vehicle check on the gang. So he'd either stolen it or had borrowed it from someone else — or he hadn't registered as the new owner of it yet.

It might be a rental.

The van backed out of the garage at around the time of night Ellie had been killed. Bethany strained to see anything inside the garage, but the light was off in there and the headlamps hadn't been switched on. The clever bastard had probably kept them off until he was well away from the street. Less chance of the beams waking the neighbours. Still, the engine might have, and if James wasn't in when they called round, she'd be knocking on some doors and asking questions.

She watched the screen again. The van drove off, the garage door closing by itself.

"Can we see the next date I gave you, please," Bethany asked.

Mrs Urshwin, in her late fifties, with an alarming blonde beehive, clicked off the current file and started a new one.

She navigated to after midnight and fast-forwarded until the van came into view again.

"And the next, please."

The woman complied, and once again, the van left in the early hours, returning a short while later. Each time matched the estimated hours of death for Ellie, Simon, and Gavin.

"Okay, go back to about six o'clock on those nights, please."

Mrs Urshwin selected the time and fast-forwarded on the most recent tape.

"Stop!" Bethany shot her hand out, pointing at the image.

With daylight still in evidence in the evening, the sun shone on the passenger side of a light-coloured car arriving.

"Can you blow that up for me?" Bethany asked. Once that was done, she looked at Mike. "Do you see who I do?"

He nodded.

Gavin in the passenger seat.

Mrs Urshwin accessed the other files and did the same. Simon had been taken to the house in the van, Ellie in the car.

Got him.

"Mrs Urshwin, do you have a memory stick you can copy those files onto for us?" Bethany smiled, trying to give the impression all was well.

"Yes," Urshwin said. "What's he done?" She slid a stick into the side of her laptop.

Play dumb. "Who?"

"James." She put her saved files from it into a new file on her laptop then clicked on the CCTV files to transfer them.

"Nothing as far as we know." Bethany hated lying, but she didn't need this lady spreading rumours around the street. Then again, people would soon realise something was up when coppers in uniform arrived.

"So why the interest then?" Urshwin took the stick out and handed it over.

Bethany slid it in her pocket. "Thanks. It's the people in his vehicles we're interested in." That would have to do.

She didn't have time to stand here fobbing her off for much longer. Or the patience. Now she knew who they were definitely after, she was desperate to leave this house and get started on finding the fucker. The problem was the nature of his business meant he could be anywhere in the city at any given time. "We'll leave you be. Thanks for the footage."

Mrs Urshwin showed them out.

On the doorstep, Bethany said to her, "Do you know if James is in?"

"His car isn't there, so I doubt it. He keeps that out on the road most of the time and the van in the garage."

"Okay." Bethany smiled and walked towards number seven. She knocked on the door once Mike stood beside her.

No answer.

"Ring him?" Mike suggested.

"I don't know. It might make him suspicious."

"Say you need to speak to him about Yazeem or Sunbeam. He won't twig it's about him then."

She knocked again. "Hmm. First, let's talk to some more neighbours. You do that side, I'll do this. Ask them if there's been any suspicious activity in the street of late. Something vague so they don't tip him off — they could be friends of his."

They split up, and Bethany went next door. A man answered, about seventy, although he appeared as though he had all his marbles, well on the sprightly side. She showed her ID, and he squinted at it.

"Hello, sir. I'm just enquiring as to whether there's been anything you'd want to report to the police." That hadn't come out right. "Sorry, let me start again. Has anything odd been going on around here?"

He pressed a finger to his chin in thought. "Only if you count him next door going out at strange hours in his new van."

"Why is that strange?"

"It isn't something he usually does. I pride myself in knowing everyone's patterns in this street — you can't be too careful. Lots of thieves about who want to steal your things. We had a couple of break-ins recently. I live alone, and as you can imagine, it's a little frightening."

"I see. When did he start this behaviour?"

"After he'd bought the van. That would be around three or four days ago. Maybe five. I can't be more exact than that."

"I see. What times stand out to you when he goes anywhere?" She knew from the footage, but him confirming it wouldn't hurt.

"It's the jaunts after midnight that annoy me. Always in the van. He's had friends there as well, which isn't unusual. They sometimes gather as a group in his house for an evening. This past week, though, it's been one friend at a time. Perhaps he's taking them home when I hear the engine — he brings them here, they don't drive themselves. One evening, I was on my way back from the corner shop when I saw them roll up."

"Okay. What time would you say he comes back?"

"Not sure. I'm in bed and don't check the clock, but I hear the rumbling and know it's him. Plus, his garage door whines a bit when it opens and closes. If it helps, it was still dark out."

"Thank you. Anything else bothering you?"

He shook his head.

"Well, thank you very much for speaking to me." She waved and walked to the neighbour on the other side. "DI Bethany Smith," she said to the woman who'd opened the door. She asked her the same as she'd asked the man.

"Yes, there was something weird." She nodded, long black hair swaying. "I can't remember what time, but I was in the back garden letting the dog out. It was late, I know that much. Anyway, there was a bang coming from James' garage, then a bash, like something had fallen and landed on the floor." She pointed to the path between their houses. "I opened my back gate and came along here, peered round to listen at the door. James was telling someone to say sorry to him."

Bethany's heart missed a beat. "Did the other person reply?"

"'No.' I went back indoors. Didn't want to get involved if he was having a row."

"And you're sure you don't know what time? Which day was it?" Bethany asked.

The neighbour scratched her head and folded her arms beneath her boobs. "A couple of nights ago. Let me think a sec . . . About eleven."

"Thank you. Do you happen to know where James might be today?"

"No, sorry. I might live next to him, but we hardly speak."

"Please may I take your name, just in case one of us needs to talk to you again?"

"Coral Marlow."

"Brilliant."

Bethany said goodbye and walked out onto the street. There weren't that many houses, but suddenly, doing door-to-door seemed a daunting task. She'd done enough of it as a uniform and hadn't much liked it then either.

Mike strode across from the other side, shaking his head, meeting her in the middle of the road. "Everyone's out except Mrs Urshwin and a fella called Bert — he didn't see or hear anything. Did you get some info?"

She nodded. "I need to knock on the other houses I was meant to be doing, but we'll talk in the car first."

They headed there and slid inside.

She explained what Coral Marlow had said. "What do you think about that?" She was hot as hell and switched the engine on so she could lower the windows.

"Sounds like he might have been talking to Simon in the garage," he said quietly, glancing about to check the street, seeing if neighbours were within earshot, no doubt.

"Might? He had to have been. The footage didn't show Simon leaving that house. Unless he left via the back and James didn't kill him, I'm thinking James wanted an apology for something or other, didn't get one, then killed him."

Her phone bleeped with a message.

Presley: WATER ANALYSIS HAS COME BACK FROM ELLIE'S AND SIMON'S LUNGS. TAP WATER WITH SOME KIND OF BATH SALTS.

Bethany: THANKS.

Presley: OH, AND SIMON HAD A CENTIPEDE DOWN HIS THROAT.

Bethany: GROSS.

She told Mike what Presley had found. "Someone has a serious relationship with insects and the like."

"The bath salts point to them being drowned in the tub," Mike said. "Maybe that's what the soap smell is on the bodies."

"Wouldn't surprise me. Nothing would at the moment. So, do we show up at his office and see if he's there?"

"Shit . . ." Mike gestured ahead.

Bethany stared through the windscreen. A silver car approached, gliding up to the kerb outside James'. She rang for backup while watching him exit the vehicle and enter his house, his head down, fists balled.

"We'll wait for help to arrive," she said, stomach clenching.

The minutes ticked by in silence. She checked the rear-view mirror and spotted a patrol car. Quickly, they got out and walked to where it had parked. Tory and Glen joined them on the path.

"For now," Bethany said, "we're just going to have a chat with him." She told them who they were going to see. "It might turn nasty, hence you being here." She quietly explained about the CCTV from Mrs Urshwin. "I'll be asking what he's doing going out in the middle of the night, so I expect either fireworks or for him to play dumb."

They trooped over the road, Bethany and Mike walking up to the door first, the others close behind. She knocked, and James answered straight away, face flushed, the knot of his tie askew.

"Oh. Hello," he said.

"Mr Obbington, we need to come in for a chat," Bethany said.

"Feel free." He swept his arm out.

"Step back, please," Mike said. "Away from the door."

James frowned as though he found that request bizarre but did as he'd been told. Was he acting, or had they assumed it was him and got the wrong person?

No. The van. The timings. Coral Marlow saying about hearing things in the garage.

Everyone entered, and James swaggered off into the kitchen. Bethany and Mike followed pretty sharpish so he didn't have a chance to grab a weapon. He hadn't. He leaned against the sink unit, arms by his sides, hands empty.

"What's up?" James asked, ignoring the fact that Tory and Glen had joined them.

The fucker isn't batting an eyelid.

"On the nights your friends were killed, we asked you where you were," Bethany said. "Why didn't you tell us that you weren't at The Ringer Hotel, and that you left this house in the middle of the night all three times? Also that you were gone around the hours people saw a Transit at Ellie's and Gavin's?"

"What does a Transit have to do with me?" He looked from one of them to the other in turn, frowning even more.

"You were seen driving one," she said. "That's what it has to do with you. A neighbour has said you bought it a few days ago."

He swallowed. "I don't know what you're talking about. I don't own a Transit."

"I think you do," Mike said, clearly pissed off with playing cat and mouse. "We'd like to look in your garage."

"You need a warrant for that." James' face displayed no emotion now. Creepy. As if he was used to wiping his expression away to hide what he was feeling.

"Fine." Mike strode out into the hall and closed the door to.

"What's he doing?" James cocked his head. Again with the creepy. His eyes turned beady, and he resembled a mad raven.

"Ringing to put in for a warrant." Bethany stared at him. "It'll take a while, but that's fine. We'll either sit outside your house until it arrives or follow you around should you choose to leave the property."

"Why do you need to follow me?"

"Actually, I'd like you to come down to the station to answer a few questions regardless."

"What about?"

"You being out in a van."

"What if I don't want to?"

She glanced at Tory and Glen.

James glanced at an internal closed door across the way.

Then bolted.

He shoved it open and flung himself into the garage, slamming the door and locking it.

"Get over there and try to open it up," Bethany said. "I'll go to the outside door." She raced out of the kitchen, dodging Mike in the hallway who had his phone pressed to his ear. "Come on. He's shut himself in the sodding garage."

Out on the drive, she headed for the garage. An engine roared to life inside, and she rushed to the large door as it rose. The damn thing went up too fast for her to lean on it and keep it semi-closed.

Filthy number plates.

She shouted for Mike to tell Tory and Glen to get in the patrol car. Having to move back, what with the door fully open now and the Transit reversing, she ran to the driver's side and tried getting in.

He'd locked up, and the van slewed in an arc, then sped off into the street. Tory and Glen legged it to their car ready to pursue while Bethany rang for a team to come to the house and guard it until the warrant came through. She ran across the road with Mike, leaped into her car and shot off after the patrol. Mike rang for uniforms to be on alert for a white Transit travelling at speed.

"Left, left, left at the end of Brollworth Mews," Tory said over the radio.

Mike replied. "Got it."

Bethany rounded the corner and spied the patrol, the Transit farther ahead. She put her foot down and caught up, overtaking patrol and flicking her lights and siren on.

"Watch yourself, your speed," Mike said. "You're closing on ninety in a residential."

"I can't let him get away. Sunbeam or Yazeem could be next, for God's sake."

She closed the distance. James swerved right onto the road that led to an industrial estate. She was relieved. Fewer people. The Transit careened around a corner and went on two wheels.

"Fuck me!" Mike shouted.

It levelled out on four wheels then, and Bethany followed, her throat tightening through adrenaline and a touch of fear. Situations like this were best left to traffic coppers, but she had no choice now but to continue the pursuit.

He came to a stop outside a large grey metal warehouse, then barrelled out of the van and ran into the building. Bethany screeched to a halt, and she flew out, Mike on her tail. As they followed James in, she caught the sound of an engine and glanced back. Tory and Glen were here.

Inside, she scoped the area. Racks and racks full of boxes, creating about forty aisles.

"James Obbington, come out, please," she called.

"Fuck off," he shouted from somewhere.

And laughed.

CHAPTER TWENTY-THREE

It was the nerves that had James laughing. That and him trying to think how the hell he could get out of this. He'd bombed it here, but that fucking Smith woman had caught up, and now look where they were. In some warehouse or other. Where were the workers? If he could find one, that'd be his meal ticket. He could use them as a body shield, a hostage, and get back to the van.

Why had he stopped here? He should have kept going.

Then he remembered why. They'd have put one of them bulletin things out on him, and every pig in the area would be on the lookout for the van.

He hadn't lied when he'd said he didn't own one. It was rented.

What did that matter now? He was in deep shit.

He moved down the aisle, towards the back of the place. Peered both ways, then headed to a metal trolley with wheels that had stuff on top. He winced at his shoes creating a racket on the floor. Switching to tiptoes, he reached the trolley. A box cutter sat on top, similar to a Stanley knife, only the blade was thinner and longer, the handle yellow plastic. That'd do. He swiped it up and ducked down the next aisle. Watched out for Smith and that Wilkins bloke.

"Obbington, it really is in your best interests to give it up now," Smith shouted. She sounded pretty far away.

He moved three aisles down.

"You're only making it worse for yourself," said Wilkins.

They must be creeping, because their footsteps were silent.

At the end of the row, he peered through a gap between some boxes, towards the doorway he'd entered through. A copper in uniform stood there, keeping guard of the exit, he reckoned. It was the woman uniform who'd been in his house, so the other bloke might be in here, too. Four of them looking for him at once.

He was going to get caught.

Voices came from his right, getting louder with every second, and he glanced in that direction. People streamed out of a doorway, heading right for him. The first in the line was some meek little female, four foot nothing, bright-yellow hair. A gaggle of others followed her, although they were a good hundred metres behind.

"So I said," one of the men was saying loudly, basically shouting, "I said, once you can do my job, you can tell me how to do it, but in the meantime, shut your cake hole."

Laughter.

The short-arse woman drew closer.

One breath. Two. Three, and he grabbed her hair and dragged her into the aisle. She screamed, hands going up to try to relax his grip, but he wasn't having any of that. He slapped his free palm over her mouth.

"I've got a knife." He waved the box cutter in front of her face and snarled in her ear, "Just do what I tell you, and everything will be fine."

She whimpered.

"Get me the fuck out of here without anyone seeing," he said. "Lead the way. You might want to avoid the coppers." He kneed her in the back — she really was fucking short — and followed her to the other end.

She rounded the corner, and Smith stood there, staring defiantly. James swung the other way, but Wilkins blocked the escape route.

"Let her go," Smith said.

James glanced back the way they'd come. The male copper was bearing down on him, some of the workers not far behind. Shit. He was surrounded.

"I call the shots," he said, staring at the box cutter in the hand that held the woman's hair. He should have put it to her throat. "Now back the fuck off. And you," he said over his shoulder to Wilkins. "Try anything, and you see this knife thing here? It'll go straight in her bloody neck."

He let go of her hair and pulled her closer, her back to his chest with his palm still over her mouth. Then lowered the blade to her throat.

"There's no need for this, James," Smith said, raising her hands like she was surrendering or some shit. Any minute now, she'd wave a white handkerchief.

"Sod off, you," he told her. "Back up."

His arm was wrenched behind him, the one with the cutter, and the woman screamed as he ripped out a chunk of her hair. She broke free, and he was wrestled to the floor, the cutter skittering off somewhere. He should have known Wilkins wouldn't do as he was told, and James was fucked off about it. He fought to shove the copper off him, but the uniformed bloke helped Wilkins out. James caught sight of the blonde, short-arse worker lunging towards Smith, and he wished he'd slit her damn neck.

The cuffs were cold on his wrists, and he couldn't deny the end had come.

He needed Pretty Princess. He needed *Bring on the Clowns*.

And, as a final humiliation, with fear setting in his marrow and chilling him from the inside out, he pissed himself.

You naughty noodle.

CHAPTER TWENTY-FOUR

Bethany and Mike sat opposite James Obbington in the interview room. He'd been deemed fit to be questioned, which gave her some satisfaction, seeing as she hadn't been able to get any answers from Timothy Bishway in her last case. He'd been taken to a secure mental facility. This one, though, this bloody James, wasn't going to get away without being talked to.

The tape and video cameras were on, recording, and Bethany waited, yet again, for him to actually answer her. She'd said several things so far that required explanation, but he hadn't even said 'no comment', just sat there, staring. His solicitor appeared bored, as though he had better things to do than be here with a murderer.

They all had better things to do. Still, this session had to continue. She wanted him to admit what he'd done.

Instead of talking about the murders this time, she decided to take a different route. "What does the gerbera mean? You left one at each of your friends' resting places."

"They stink," he said.

At last, he speaks.

"Don't you like the smell?" She held back a yawn. It had been a long hour of waiting for him to talk, and tiredness had got the better of her.

He stared at the closed file on the table in front of Bethany. Inside were images of his friends, dead, something she intended to use to push him into a confession later if he didn't start bleating now. They'd been taken off his phone. The creepy fuck had snapped images after he'd left them in their gardens.

"No," he said. "Reminds me of . . ."

She jumped on that right away. "Who does it remind you of?"

"Her."

"Who is her?"

"That bitch."

"Who is that bitch?"

"Gelly." He laughed then, a bit on the crackers side, like he was one player short of a game of solitaire. "Gelly. What a prick, calling her that."

He thought of himself as a prick?

Confused, she prodded, "Who is Gelly?" She sat up straighter. Him giving what she assumed was a name had somewhat perked her up.

"Find out for yourself. It's your job."

Earlier, after James had been brought in, Fran and Leona had looked deeper into his past. He'd been adopted by an aunt after his mother had died. It clicked then, who he'd meant.

"Angelica?" She let the word hang there, a spectre, and a frightening one at that, going by his reaction.

His face paled, and the smirk disappeared. "Yeah, her." He said meekly. A different person, not the usual, confident James.

"Why is she a bitch?" Bethany sipped some water, then wished she hadn't. She'd need the loo soon and didn't want to leave the room now James had decided to have a conversation.

"The garden. The shed."

"What about them?"

"She left me there."

Was that why he'd put his friends in *their* gardens? She asked him just that.

"None of your business," he said.

She thought about telling him it *was* her business, but he might clam up again, get belligerent.

Try something else. "What about the insects, the blue butterfly? What do they mean?"

"It all relates to the garden and the shed. Bit obvious, isn't it?"

"So you were in the garden and the shed with insects?"

"That big-nostrilled cow put them in there with me."

Big-nostrilled cow? "Who, Angelica?"

"Who else?"

"Why did she do that?"

"I don't fucking know, do I? She kept saying they were my friends, but the only friend I had was Pretty Princess at first, until I met the gang."

"Who is Pretty Princess?"

"She's in a box."

Oh my fucking God. "Where?" she said, more urgently than she'd intended. She didn't want to spook him and make him retreat into silence, but it was too late to take it back.

He smiled a secret smile. "At my house."

No one had reported back to her that a body had been found at his place.

"In your garden?" she asked. Had he buried some poor woman out there?

"No, the shed."

Mike got his phone out and typed a message.

Bethany continued. "Okay, is Pretty Princess dead?"

"No, she can still dance. She's old, but the box still works."

What the fucking hell is he on about? "What box?"

"The jewellery box, you dopey fucking tart. She's the ballerina inside." He hummed a tune, closing his eyes, lines of stress smoothing out on his forehead.

Bethany scoured her brain for the title of the song. Nothing. She recognised it, though, so maybe it would come to her soon.

"Why the makeup?" She hid a shudder at how hideous the faces had looked.

"Clowns."

Bring on the Clowns. She suppressed a shudder. "What about them?"

"Gelly and that bloke. They were clowns when their faces joined together."

Faces joined together? "I don't understand what you mean. Can you explain for me?"

"They joined. He had blue eyeshadow, and she had a moustache."

"Is that why you put blue eyeshadow and drew moustaches on Simon and Gavin?"

He shrugged.

"The game mouthpiece," she said. "What's that about?"

"Stopped me hearing them properly, didn't it. Made their words all distorted so I didn't know what they said."

"Did you make them wear them before they were killed then?"

"No. After."

Yes! He's confessed. "I see. But if they're dead, they can't speak anyway, so why bother."

"Symbolism. Doesn't matter. They needed to be there."

"Why did you kill them?"

"They laughed at me."

"What for?"

"I told them about nostril woman. They thought it was funny. Abuse isn't funny."

Bethany's stomach went south. "Tell me about it?"

"Will you laugh?"

"Of course not." Why would she?

He talked properly then, everything spilling out, and by the time he'd finished, Bethany was hard pressed to keep tears from falling. She wiped them away, but not before James had seen them. The red dress and shoes made sense, the blue suit, the red tie, Simon with his shirt done up, Gavin's undone. What a mess.

"I'm very sorry you went through that," she said.

"You're sorry?" He blinked, nonplussed.

"Yes. No child should have to endure that."

"You said sorry . . ." He stared around, seemingly bewildered. "That was all I ever wanted."

She thought of what Coral Marlow had said about James asking someone to say sorry in his garage. "Did you want your friends to say it?"

He nodded, eyes glistening.

"What about Polly Dilway. Why did you kill her?"

"She saw the van." His anger returned, setting his slack face into a hard mask. He slapped the table, glaring at Bethany.

"I think we need to take a break," she said. "James Obbington, I am arresting you for the murders of . . ."

* * *

Bethany sat in Sunbeam's house, on a chair beneath the living room window. Sunbeam and Yazeem were opposite on the sofa. Mike stood by the door. This was a courtesy visit, to tell them who had killed their friends. It could have been done on the phone, but Bethany wanted to tell them herself.

While everyone got settled, she thought about the call she'd recently had from Isabelle. Ellie's, Simon's, and Gavin's clothes and shoes had been found in James' house, as well as their tongues, dried out in the drawer of a Welsh dresser. The 'box' had been one used for jewellery, and Pretty Princess must have been the ballerina inside. Even if he hadn't confessed, they'd have enough evidence against him. Forensics had come back saying the blue water had Radox bath salts in it, and that was what the bodies had been scented with. He'd used blue bubble bath in Polly's spa.

She shook the thoughts out of her head.

The half full coffee cup warmed her hands, so she placed it on the table. While the sun still raged, even though it was early evening, she was hot and bothered after spending all those hours in the interview room with James. It was well past clocking-off time, but she just wanted this over and done with. Tomorrow, all the paperwork and evidence collating would take her attention.

"We've found who did it," she said, "which is why I wanted you here together."

"Who?" Sunbeam asked, grabbing Yazeem's hand.

"I'm afraid it was James." Bethany gave what she hoped was a sympathetic look.

"You're kidding." Yazeem stared from Bethany to Sunbeam then back again. "James? Why?"

"The reason he gave was that you all needed to say sorry or be sorry."

"Sorry for what?" Sunbeam shook her head.

"For his childhood. He said he told you all what had happened, and everyone laughed."

Sunbeam blushed. Yazeem stared down at her lap.

"Did you?" Bethany asked.

Sunbeam nodded. "We thought he was joking. It was one of those moments where we were telling childhood secrets, and honestly, it was so off-the-wall, it sounded like he'd made it up."

"From what he told me," Bethany said, "I'm inclined to believe him. I think he got broken along the way somewhere — which isn't surprising at all, given what he endured — and right and wrong got muddied. He felt you all needed to pay for laughing, and the result was murder."

Isabelle had let Bethany know that a foot spa had been found in James' garage, a box of Radox beside it. It was currently with forensics, but it was a safe bet that James had drowned his friends in it.

"God, we could have been next if you hadn't caught him," Yazeem said.

"Yes, he admitted as much." She'd spoken to him again before leaving the station. She'd put a bet on it that these two were counting their lucky stars right this minute.

"Fuck." Sunbeam fiddled with her ponytail, winding the end around her finger. "We shouldn't have taken the piss out of him. God, I feel so bad."

"But he killed our friends," Yazeem said.

"Maybe take this as a massive lesson in watching how you react to people who share secrets in the future," Bethany said. "You never know what they're going through in order to survive, to get past it." What she hadn't said lingered in the air: If you'd shown compassion instead of laughing, he might not have killed anyone.

She took a few more sips of coffee, then rose. It had been a long day.

Bethany and Mike left the house, and she took him home.

"Do you want company tonight?" he asked, unbuckling his seat belt. "I can nip in and get a bag, clean clothes and whatnot for tomorrow."

That sounded like something she could handle. Being alone in that house wasn't enjoyable in the least. "Okay, you go in and get sorted. I've got something I need to do, so I'll do it, then come back for you."

Mike got out, and she drove off. She hadn't had time to visit Vinny since the day of the funeral, and while that might have been a good thing, she had the urge to go and talk to him.

She pulled up at the cemetery and, thankful it was still open — summer hours — she made her way to his grave. For some reason, she was shocked to find it filled in. Last she'd seen it, his coffin had been visible, and she'd stared down at his shiny name plaque, telling him she wished she was in there with him. While life without him was hard — too bloody hard for words — after working this case, she had some direction now. She'd promised him she'd throw herself into her job because that was what he'd want, and she had.

"Well, Vin," she said, wishing he could hear her wherever he was. "I went back to work earlier than intended, which is why I haven't nipped by to see you. And we caught the bastard. Not before he'd killed a fair few people, mind, but we got him all the same."

She waited for an answer, then berated herself for expecting one. Vin wasn't going to say 'Well done, love' or

'I'm so proud of you'. She'd just have to tell herself he'd be thinking it in spirit, nudging her on towards a future without him. And he would do that. He'd want her to move along and be happy. It was a bit too soon for her to be as happy as she was when he'd been alive, but maybe one day she'd get there, although a part of her would always be sad.

"I'm going to have to move out of the house," she said quickly, as though it would hurt his feelings if she said it slower. "Not because I don't love the place, or because I don't care about the memories, but it's too difficult to stay. If I don't leave, I'll go mental. Hope you don't mind."

A slight breeze ruffled the flowers covering the mound of mud.

It was him, wasn't it?

"Mike's looking after me, you'll be glad to know," she said. "He's staying again tonight. It gets a bit lonely without you. No funny business, though. We're just mates."

She chattered on for a little while longer, then said she'd see him soon, in her dreams, in everything that reminded her of him — the scent of his aftershave, the feel of his fleece, the echo of his laughter, so many things.

The walk to the car didn't pain her as much as it had last time, and she supposed that was the way grief ticked. You got on. You made your new life work.

She drove to Mike's and picked him up, then went to the local chippy and ordered them some dinner. She bought herself a chicken and mushroom Pukka pie, chips, and gravy, exactly what Vinny had got her before. The lump in her throat could do with buggering off, but she managed to pay and return to the car without bawling.

It was going to be a long road, with potholes on the way, but she'd keep going.

There was nothing else left to do, was there?

At her house, they ate, had a few glasses of wine, and she told Mike about moving to a new home.

"Not out of the city, I hope," he said.

"No, just to a smaller place."

A photo of Vinny tumbled off the mantelpiece, his smiling face beaming up at her from the floor.

Bethany smiled, too, remembering.

He'd always said if he died before her, he'd give her the thumbs-up by throwing something. God love that man. He'd given her his blessing.

THE END

THE JOFFE BOOKS STORY

We began in 2014 when Jasper agreed to publish his mum's much-rejected romance novel and it became a bestseller.

Since then we've grown into the largest independent publisher in the UK. We're extremely proud to publish some of the very best writers in the world, including Joy Ellis, Faith Martin, Caro Ramsay, Helen Forrester, Simon Brett and Robert Goddard. Everyone at Joffe Books loves reading and we never forget that it all begins with the magic of an author telling a story.

We are proud to publish talented first-time authors, as well as established writers whose books we love introducing to a new generation of readers.

We have been shortlisted for Independent Publisher of the Year at the British Book Awards three times, in 2020, 2021 and 2022, and for the Diversity and Inclusivity Award at the Independent Publishing Awards in 2022.

We built this company with your help, and we love to hear from you, so please email us about absolutely anything bookish at: feedback@joffebooks.com.

If you want to receive free books every Friday and hear about all our new releases, join our mailing list: www.joffebooks.com/contact

And when you tell your friends about us, just remember: it's pronounced Joffe as in coffee or toffee!

ALSO BY EMMY ELLIS

DI BETHANY SMITH
Book 1: THE COLD CALL KILLER
Book 2: THE CREEPY-CRAWLY KILLER

DETECTIVE CAROL WREN MYSTERIES
Book 1: SPITE YOUR FACE
Book 2: HOLD YOUR BREATH
Book 3: GUILT BURNS HOLES
Book 4: BEST SERVED COLD
Book 5: BLOOD RUNS DEEP

Printed in Great Britain
by Amazon

60207609R00109